His AMISH BRIDE

Dorothy Clarans

Annie's®

AnniesFiction.com

Library of Congress-in-Publication Data
His Amish Bride / by Dorothy Clarans
p. cm.
ISBN: 979-8-89253-195-5
I. Title
                              2019935019

AnniesFiction.com
(800) 282-6643
Hearts of Amish Country™
Series Creator: Shari Lohner
Series Editor: Jane Haertel

10 11 12 13 14 | Printed in China | 9 8 7 6 5 4

1

Candace Beachey wondered if today was the day the bishop would give her *Daed* an ultimatum. He had missed church yesterday and his absence had been noted. Again. While the bread was browning in the oven, she called up the stairs, "Daed? Breakfast."

She didn't have high hopes that he would come down, but she went through the routine of it anyway, which gave her some comfort. She'd probably wind up delivering a tray to his bedroom, as she had for the past three months. He had taken *Mamm*'s death hard, losing interest in life and his faith. Candace worried about him constantly. Something had to be done, but she didn't know what that was.

Candace had been up for hours doing his chores and hers in the frigid January morning. After tending to the animals, she still had more to do before she went to her job at the Randolph Amish Market. The thought of her Nigerian goats prancing excitedly this morning made her smile. Her brother Simon and her nephew Gabriel, who lived next door, had built an igloo for them to climb on. The goats often made a game of darting in and out and bouncing all around the icy structure.

She filled the percolator and set it to boil while she put bacon in the frying pan. Bacon and coffee. Who could resist? Cocking her head, Candace listened, but she didn't hear any movement from upstairs. Her Mamm would never come down those steps again. The grief was still as fresh as it had been on the day they buried her, an aching wound that had crippled her father and nearly broken her.

The front door opened, and she heard boots come clomping in.

Candace wasn't surprised when Simon and Gabriel came into the kitchen. Judging by the mess they were tracking, they had probably walked through the snow and mud instead of along the plowed road. She could almost hear her mother calling, "Take off your boots!"

Candace sighed. She'd have to wash the floor after work. There wouldn't be time this morning. She just hoped no one would stop by before she could clean.

"Do you need anything?" Simon asked.

"*Nee. Denki.*" Candace smiled at her brother. "Thank you for finishing the shoveling while I was at work yesterday."

"I'm just glad we didn't have another storm last night."

Candace nodded. Her back was still aching from clearing out the driveway. "Do you want some *Kaffi*?"

"I wouldn't say no to a cup." Simon sat down at the table.

"Have you eaten?" she asked her nephew.

"*Ja*," he said.

"Do you think you can help me out with some of this bacon anyway? I made too much."

Gabriel's face broke out into a wide grin. "Ja."

Candace fried up some eggs, slathered some toast with her freshly made butter, and made sandwiches with the bacon for the three of them. She made a fourth one and set out a place at the table, as she always did, just in case.

She poured Simon a cup of coffee and Gabriel a glass of milk and joined them at the table. It was *gut* to have a family breakfast. Simon led the morning prayer and tears gathered in her eyes. She had missed this. Her father refused to pray now, and since he hadn't been to church since her mother died, Candace was terrified the bishop was going to excommunicate him, and he would be shunned from their Amish community.

"How's Daed?" Simon asked in a low voice.

"The same."

"I'll have Esther look in on him this afternoon."

"Why? Where are you going today?" she asked. His wife was almost due with their third *Boppli*, and the current baby, Abraham, had just learned to walk. Candace was sure, though, that he had skipped over walk and gone straight to run.

Simon was a carpenter and woodworker like their father, and since everything was covered in snow and ice, building jobs were few and far between in Randolph, New York. He had been a great help with Daed this winter. Candace didn't have to feel guilty about leaving Daed alone because Simon would come over in the afternoon and convince him to go next door and visit with his grandchildren. Then, between him and Esther, they would make sure he ate a proper meal surrounded by family. Of course, by the time she got back from work, Daed would be back up in his room, and she would spend another lonely meal by herself.

"I got a job," he said with a broad grin on his face.

"That's wonderful. Doing what?" She said a quick prayer of gratitude. Money had been tight this winter.

"There's an abandoned strip mall in Corry, Pennsylvania, that the new owners are renovating. They contacted a Mennonite company to gather a bunch of workers from around here to help get the project ready for the spring. They need all the help they can get."

"Pennsylvania?" Candace frowned. "Isn't that a long way to go for a job?"

He hunched his shoulders. "It's a little over an hour going by car. The Mennonite company leased a van. They're making several stops in Randolph to pick up a bunch of us. It's not like we can earn money here, in this weather."

She winced at the frustration in his voice. "Is there anything I can do to help?"

"Actually, there is." Simon rubbed the back of his neck. "Esther isn't feeling well. I'm taking Gabriel out of school today, so he can watch me and learn."

"I get to carry the tools. I hope Daed lets me use the hammer."

"We'll see," Simon said. Turning to Candace, he said, "This way, if she needs to rest in the afternoon, she won't have to worry about taking care of him after school."

"I can take care of myself," Gabriel said.

Gabriel was growing up so fast, Candace couldn't believe it. In another few years, he'd be done with school and learning a trade. She felt as if he'd been Abraham's age only yesterday. Her mother would have loved to see him now, going to work with his father. She blinked back tears and abruptly stood up.

"Do you need me to pack your lunches?" Candace asked, eager to help and keep the sad feelings away.

"If you can. I'd rather not spend the money eating out, though I'm sure there would be some place to buy lunch if we needed to."

"Of course I will. If you want, I can take off work and help Esther today." Her boss wouldn't like that so much, but Candace's family had to come first. They were all she had left.

"Esther will be fine. She just needs to rest until the sickness passes. She's drinking peppermint tea and eating crackers now."

"I don't have any lunch meat, but I can make some egg salad. The hens were very generous today. And I think I can throw in some brownies that I made yesterday." Candace winked at her nephew, who grinned widely at her.

"That sounds perfect as long as it's not too much trouble."

"Nonsense," Candace said, briskly. "I'll go set the eggs to boil. And you can tell me more about this job."

She lit the burner and set a pot filled with water on it. A creak from upstairs gave her some hope, so she said louder than she had to, "I bet they have a lot of work, if they're sending a van for our carpenters."

Simon took her lead and raised his own voice. "It's decent pay too. They're looking to remodel the strip mall and make it a children's center. The owner is a contractor, so this could lead to more jobs."

"That would be such a blessing," she said. While the eggs boiled, Candace chopped an onion, some celery, and a bell pepper, then mixed them with mayonnaise and mustard. After adding in a pinch of sugar, a splash of vinegar, and a shake of salt, pepper, and celery seed, she was ready for the eggs once they finished cooking.

She refilled her brother's coffee cup and then collected the dirty dishes. Placing them in the sink, she spotted the leftover bacon. She had been so sure that the coffee and bacon would work some magic on her father. She crumbled that into the egg salad mixture. She heard a creak on the stairs and froze in place. Was he coming down, after all?

Swallowing hard, she peeked over her shoulder to see if Simon had heard it. Judging by how wide his eyes were, he had.

Candace cleared her throat. "I hope they won't turn you away if there are too many carpenters."

Simon nodded, understanding that she was trying to catch her father's interest. "Well, if they do, it will be a wasted day, traveling back and forth for nothing."

"Is the pay even worth it?"

"Ja, it'll be enough to get us through the rest of the winter with a little left over besides."

Candace held her breath until she heard footsteps on the stairs. She and Simon exchanged looks of cautious hope.

A few seconds later, her father shambled into the kitchen and stared at them blearily with empty eyes. He was a shadow of himself, but at least he was dressed and downstairs. When he sat down at the table, Candace raced to get him some coffee and fry some more eggs.

"Just coffee soup today," he said, his voice cracking from misuse.

She was about to argue, but Simon subtly shook his head at her. "All right, Daed," she said. Lemuel Beachey was a proud and stubborn man. If she rubbed him the wrong way, he could very well go back upstairs.

Candace toasted some more bread and cut it into chunks, which she set in the bottom of a cereal bowl. She poured in coffee, milk, and a few heaping teaspoons of sugar. She didn't care for coffee soup herself, but her father loved it. She finished it with a dash of cinnamon and brought it to the table with more slices of bread and butter. If she had known he would choose today to come downstairs, she would have made his favorite—blueberry muffins. She would pick up the ingredients at work today and make them for him tomorrow.

When he started eating as if he hadn't spent most of the last three months upstairs curled into a ball, Candace slumped in relief. He was coming back to them. It was all right if he wasn't speaking or making conversation. It was enough that he was here. She should run upstairs and freshen up his room while she had the chance, but she was hesitant to leave the table.

"I've got to go," Simon said with clear reluctance. "The van should be here soon."

"Need an extra hand?" Daed asked.

Candace caught her breath.

"Uh, yes, absolutely," Simon said. "The more hands the better."

"Do we have any bologna?" Lemuel picked up his bowl and polished off the rest of his breakfast.

"Nee." She got up from the table. "But the eggs should be ready by now. I'll make you all egg salad sandwiches."

"Make me two. And a thermos of coffee."

"Ja, Daed." She wasn't sure what had caused the change in him, but she wasn't going to question it. "Simon, can you hook up my buggy so I'm not late for work?"

"Sure. We still have a few minutes before the van will arrive."

"I'll go with you," her father said. "My tools are in the barn."

She ran out to the back porch, scooped a pile of snow into a pot, and brought it into the house. Her father was putting on his boots and winter coat when she raced back into the kitchen.

With a slotted spoon, she plopped the hot eggs into the snow to chill them quickly so she could peel them without burning her hands.

Through the kitchen window, she saw Simon hitching her horse, Belle, to the buggy. She opened the window. "How much time do I have?" she called to him. She rifled through the cupboard until she found a large picnic basket.

"We might have to leave without the sandwiches," Simon called back. "I'm sure we can buy lunch from somewhere. Don't worry about it."

Candace could almost feel her mother rolling over in her grave. She couldn't replace her mother, but she could make the hole Mamm had left in their lives a little bit smaller. "Nee," she said firmly. "If you have to leave, go. I'll catch up with you in the buggy. You said the van was going farm to farm?"

"You can't catch up to a car," Gabriel said.

"Have you seen the way your *Aenti* drives?" Simon teased.

"Oh, stop. I'm assuming they're going to stop at the Eicher farm?" The three Eicher boys were all carpenters and woodworkers. She poured the pot of coffee into a thermos.

"Probably," Simon said.

"Great. I'll go through the Millers' farm and take the cow trail. I should meet you there." Candace added the whole pan of brownies and three apples and oranges to the basket. She wished they had potato chips.

"Is it even plowed?"

"He's the bishop. Of course it's plowed. And the Eichers' farm is the next one over." She started another pot of coffee. She'd give them two thermoses. Candace wished her mother was here. She would have been able to put this together in no time.

"Maybe I shouldn't do this," Lemuel said, coming up to Simon with his toolbox.

"Nee!" Simon and Candace said at the same time. Candace wanted everything to be perfect. She wanted things to be the way they used to be. Her Mamm would never send him off without a homemade lunch, and Candace wouldn't either.

Simon looked over his shoulder at his farm. Esther was on the porch waving a blue shirt. "Your buggy is all set. But either the van is coming or Esther wants me to change my shirt. I'm taking Daed and Gabriel back home to wait for the van in either case. Don't worry if you can't make it."

"I can do this," she insisted before she shut the window. With shaking fingers, she started peeling the eggs. When she was a girl, her Mamm would challenge her to get the eggshell off in one piece. Mamm had been a master at it and, eventually, Candace could do it too. But she wasn't about to waste time with that today.

Finally, she chopped the eggs, then slid them into the bowl with the vegetables and added the dressing. She made eight sandwiches because it was a long trip to Pennsylvania and back. She had just finished when she heard a horn beep from next door.

"Oh no!" she whispered, closing the picnic basket. She poured the coffee into the second thermos and added cream and sugar.

Candace threw on her coat, tied on her bonnet, and hurried outside with the heavy basket. The van was already pulling away down the street. Launching herself into the buggy, she grabbed the reins and encouraged Belle to stretch her legs. Candace guided her down the road until they got to the Millers' farm and headed up the plowed driveway. As she passed the farmhouse, she waved at her friend Betsy Miller as she sped by, the buggy bouncing on the packed snow. Out of the corner of her eye, she saw that Betsy's father, the bishop, had also come out on the porch to see what all the fuss was.

She'd worry about that later.

She crossed over into the Eichers' property just as the van pulled up and beeped its horn. She sprinted to the van, but the toe of her boot caught on some uneven ice and she went down.

Strong arms caught her just before she hit the ground.

She and her rescuer staggered and almost went into a snowdrift, but he planted his feet and they rocked to a stop. She didn't even lose her grip on the extra thermos or the picnic basket.

"Denki," she panted and lifted her eyes up to her savior. She had been expecting one of the Eicher boys, with whom she had gone to school, and was prepared for a good-natured teasing. Instead, she looked up and saw a handsome stranger. He had warm brown eyes and an easy smile. His dark hair was blowing in his face, because, while they hadn't landed in the snowbank, his black felt hat had.

"Aenti Candace, you made it!" Gabriel crowed. He jumped out of the van and grabbed the lunch items from her.

She had been staring up at the stranger for longer than was proper and she was still half in his arms. She freed herself, hoping she could blame her blush on the cold air.

"Denki," she said again.

"Are you all right?" His voice was deep and rich. It reminded her of warm caramel, and she shivered.

"I'm fine."

"You didn't twist your ankle?" His eyes sparkled warmly.

"Nee." She was grinning like a fool, but she couldn't stop.

The van blasted its horn again, and the man reluctantly stepped away from her.

"Bring home some bologna," her father called from the van.

"I will." She waved. Her heart was still racing and she was feeling a bit dizzy.

The man retrieved his hat from the snow and dusted it off. He tipped it at her with a grin, then hopped into the van. Candace stared dumbly after the vehicle as it drove away. When she snapped herself out of her trance, she turned and saw her mother's friend Judy Eicher watching her with a raised eyebrow.

"What was that all about?"

"Esther's sick and Daed decided to go to work with Simon. I was running late this morning, so I had to meet them here to give them their lunch." Candace shrugged.

"You almost broke your neck," Judy scolded. "You're lucky Micah was there."

"Micah?"

"Micah Zehr. He's my sister's boy from Pennsylvania."

"What's he doing here in Randolph?"

"Looking for work, same as everyone else. His Daed is a minister. I think he wants Micah to find someone to marry here and then go back home to start a farm and family. I'm hoping he sticks around."

Candace grinned. "You've got three boys already. What are you going to do with a fourth one?"

"There are always more chores to do."

"That's very true," Candace agreed ruefully.

"Fortunately, Bishop Mark seems to have taken a liking to the young man. It's possible your friend Betsy might make a nice match for him. I was hoping to introduce them at a frolic sometime soon."

If her father was pushing for it, Betsy would definitely consider courting Micah. She was terrified of disappointing her Daed. *It must be difficult when your father is the bishop.*

"I'd like to do some ice skating," Candace said. "I'm sure the pond is well frozen. I'll have to check with Esther and see if she's feeling up to hosting a frolic." She climbed back into the buggy.

"Do you think they would be a good match?" Judy pressed, looking at her with a hopeful expression.

Candace took a moment to catch her breath. "Betsy is a good friend and a good person. She'd make anyone an excellent wife." It was true, and it was the right thing to say—so why did it feel wrong to think about Micah and Betsy? She had barely met the man.

"Speaking of good matches, I think my Amos will be asking you to step out soon."

"Amos?" Candace had to choke back a laugh. She liked him well enough. But she'd never thought of him as more than a friend.

"I told him it was too soon after your Mamm's passing. But I wanted you to know, to give you a little ray of sunshine in your dark days."

She had nothing against Amos, but if he had wanted to step out with her, he would have asked before now.

"I shouldn't have said anything," Judy continued. "You should get to work."

"I'll see you later, Judy."

Candace guided the horse down the Eichers' driveway and took a more sedate pace to the Randolph Amish Market where she worked. For months now, every time she made this journey, all she had really wanted to do was go home, crawl back into bed, and toss the quilt over her head. But this morning, as the winter sunshine warmed her face and Belle trotted along, she couldn't help thinking things might just be looking up.

2

Micah Zehr watched the snow angel talk to his Aenti until the van turned onto the road and he couldn't see her anymore. Her eyes sparkled, and he'd caught a glimpse of shiny brown hair peeking out from under her *Kapp*. Her pink cheeks and radiant smile had made his heart stutter. He hoped he would see her again soon. Settling back into his seat, he saw two men eyeing him sternly and a little boy beaming up at him.

Aenti Candace, the boy had called her. Judging by the age and family resemblance, these men were her brother and father. They seemed to be waiting on something. Maybe an introduction.

"I'm Micah Zehr. I'm staying with my cousins." He indicated the three Eicher boys, who had promptly leaned back into their seats for a nap.

"I'm Simon Beachey. This is my Dacd, Lemuel, and my son Gabriel. And that," the younger of the two men said, pointing out the window, "was my sister Candace."

"Thank you for keeping her from falling," Lemuel added, before he turned to gaze at the scenery flashing by.

Micah didn't think it would be appropriate to say it had been his pleasure, so he just nodded. She had smelled like fresh air and vanilla. He wished he'd had the time to have a conversation with her. But her buggy had barreled onto the farm as if she were being chased by a bear, and then he'd had to leave all too soon in the van.

"Why was she in such a hurry?"

"She wanted to make sure we had our lunch," Simon explained. "My wife's ill and it was last minute."

Micah was impressed. "That's dedication."

"She almost broke her neck," Simon said sourly.

"*Gött* was watching out for her," Micah said.

Lemuel grunted and crossed his arms in front of him.

"Where are you from?" Simon coughed, then shifted his body to block Micah's view of Lemuel.

Micah wondered why Simon was doing that. Perhaps he was afraid his father would call Micah to task for being so forward with his daughter. He really hadn't had a chance to think about it. He just hadn't wanted her to hurt herself.

"Autumnfield. It's a few miles south of Lancaster in Pennsylvania."

"Most people would go south rather than north during January."

Micah laughed. "I wouldn't know what to do with myself if there wasn't cold and snow. My Aenti told me about this job, and it's easier to live here than it is to commute from home."

"It's nice to meet you," Simon said. "Welcome."

"Denki. I'm looking forward to seeing how maple syrup is made. My cousins have been telling me all about it and have already given me a tour of their sugar shack."

"Next month, depending on the weather."

They settled into their seats and watched the scenery go by. Micah should probably take advantage of the time for a short nap like his cousins, but he couldn't stop thinking about Candace Beachey and her beautiful eyes.

He hadn't come to Randolph for romance, though. He'd come for a steady paycheck and to escape his father's constant assumptions that he would start a tobacco or grain farm. His father had promised him fifty acres once he got married.

The only problem was, Micah didn't want to be a farmer.

Micah liked working with wood and creating things with his hands. Farming was all well and good. It kept them fed during the winter, but it wasn't what made him feel closer to Gött. Building things did. He was especially interested in making kitchen cabinets. There was a lot of demand for that, and while he had experience with carpentry and woodworking, he wanted to specialize and hone his skills.

His father had also mentioned that Micah had a lot in common with Bishop Mark's daughter. Which he couldn't possibly know, so it was his subtle way of telling Micah to start looking for a bride. Betsy seemed nice enough, though they'd barely met. However, as with the girls back home, he hadn't felt any kind of connection with her. Micah supposed he should give her a chance, but this morning his mind kept drifting back to Candace. He felt like he had been kicked in the gut by a mule when their eyes met and he was now only beginning to recover from it.

Pulling out his prayer book, he tried to read, but he wasn't comprehending, so he closed it again and leaned his forehead against the cool window. He wished his father could understand that he didn't want to be a farmer like his brothers. Aenti Judy had raised a whole brood of carpenters and they were doing just fine. Although, her husband had fallen off a scaffold and died on a jobsite. Maybe his father was worried the same would happen to him. But there was danger in all professions. You couldn't hide from Gött's will. If He called you home, it didn't matter where you were or what you were doing at the time.

His thoughts drifted toward his youngest sister, who had answered that call. She had taken ill and the sickness had turned into pneumonia. Micah didn't understand why it had happened so quickly and wondered if anyone could have prevented it. Was that what his father was doing with his demands on Micah's life? Trying to control the inevitable?

Micah knew Sarah was with Gött and free from any mortal strife, but he missed her just the same. Daed never spoke about it, but Micah knew he missed his youngest daughter too.

The van ride was long, and he was glad to get out and stretch when they finally got there. The wind kicked up and blew through his jacket as he made his way inside the building with the rest of the workers. The foreman put them to work immediately in various parts of the mall. Micah had a chance to glance at the plans, which were displayed on a tripod, while he was waiting to be assigned. This place would be nice for *Kinner* to play in when they were done. And the work for the men should last until spring.

Micah and the other unmarried men were assigned to clearing out the waste products and debris because the dust masks fit their clean-shaven faces better. He had been hoping to be on the framing team, but there was more than enough work to go around. It was going to be a long day. Between him and his cousins, the nightly chores when they got home wouldn't take long, but he wondered how the men with smaller families would make out.

On their first break, he realized that he had left his lunch in the van. He didn't see the vehicle in the parking lot so he found Lou, the foreman. He was a stocky *Englischer* who had a cigar in the corner of his mouth and his cell phone permanently stuck to his ear, it seemed.

Micah waited patiently for him to finish his conversation. He couldn't tell if Lou was angry at the person he was talking with or if that was his normal tone of voice.

When he hung up, he fixed Micah with a sharp eye. "What can I do for you, kid?"

"Do you know where the van is? I left my lunch there."

"Driver won't be back until five thirty. There's a doughnut shop down the street, but you won't be able to make it there and back on break." Lou squinted around. "I think there's some coffee on that table."

"Thank you." Micah didn't really want the coffee, but he hadn't had anything since breakfast. He tried to catch his cousins' eyes, but they weren't on the same break schedule as he was. He wasn't about to take from their lunches and leave them short. Aunt Judy was having trouble making ends meet, and until they all got their first paychecks, meals would be lean.

He sipped the tepid, stale coffee while sitting on the steps of the strip mall. It was cold, but the fresh air was worth it. He tried to envision the Kinner coming in and playing. The poster board called it a "science and discovery center." He wasn't entirely sure what that entailed, but it sounded like a place that combined learning with play. He liked the idea.

The Beacheys came outside too. They sat next to him and opened the gigantic picnic basket.

"Would you like a brownie? Candace packed enough for an army," Simon said.

He did, but he knew that basket had to feed three people. One of whom was a young boy. Gabriel was peering into the basket eagerly.

"Nee," he said. "Denki."

Lemuel shrugged and unwrapped a large pan of brownies, then removed one that looked particularly thick and dense.

Micah laughed. "You weren't kidding."

Lemuel silently offered him one, and there seemed to be plenty, so he took it. After tasting his first bite, he closed his eyes in satisfaction. In addition to being beautiful and a little bit reckless, Candace could bake too.

"She puts in *Grossmammi's* secret ingredient," Gabriel said as he tucked into a brownie with gusto. "Do you want to know what it is?"

"It wouldn't be a secret then." Micah grinned at the boy.

"I feel like I can trust you. You won't tell anybody, will you?"

"Not a soul." He exchanged glances with Simon, who grinned at his son. Lemuel stared into the distance.

Gabriel leaned forward and lowered his voice confidentially, his serious expression spoiled by a bit of chocolate on his cheek. "Instant coffee. She says that's what brings out the chocolate flavor."

Micah took another bite and chewed thoughtfully, trying to taste the coffee, but he couldn't. However, they did taste particularly chocolatey, and maybe that was because of the coffee as Gabriel claimed. "Please tell her that they are delicious."

"I will."

Lemuel refilled his own cup and Micah's from the large thermos in the basket.

"She'll appreciate it," Simon said. "It hasn't been easy for her since Mamm died last fall."

Micah had guessed their mother had passed, if Candace was acting as the woman of the house, but he was shocked to learn it had been so recent. "I'm sorry for your loss," he said genuinely.

"Me too." Simon looked down and frowned. "It's strange without her. Some days, I feel like she's right next to me. Other times, it's like she was never here at all. I don't know which one is worse."

"I know how you feel." Micah had a hard time swallowing, but the coffee was strong and it soothed his throat, pushing back the familiar grief.

"You've lost a wife?" Lemuel asked with an edge to his voice.

"Nee, my baby sister, Sarah."

"Sarah?" Lemuel blinked at him in shock. "Sarah was my wife's name." He cleared his throat. "Heart attack."

"Pneumonia." That was all he could get out. Sarah was a common name in Amish communities, but the coincidence still made him feel a kindred grief with the Beacheys.

"*Ach*," Lemuel said, laying a heavy hand on Micah's back. "I'm sorry for your loss as well. This world is an unforgiving place full of sorrow and pain."

Micah took a shaky breath. "It can seem that way, ja."

"How did your parents handle her death?" Simon asked. "I couldn't even imagine . . ." He clasped Gabriel's shoulder, but the boy was concentrating on his brownie, apparently oblivious to the adult conversation going on around him.

"The only way we knew how. We went on. The sun still came up. There were still chores to do. My Daed spent a lot of time in his garden, and my Mamm worked herself harder than I thought anyone could. It still hurts. I think it always will. But our faith comforted us, as I'm sure yours comforts you."

Lemuel just grunted.

"I like to build things—that's work I enjoy—but I don't get the chance to do it back home. Daed's determined to make a farmer out of me."

"No reason you can't do both," Simon suggested, then glanced at Lemuel as if to see if he would respond.

Micah was puzzled by the hopeful expectation in Simon's eyes, as if he *needed* his Daed to speak. Maybe if he said the right thing, he could encourage Lemuel, who was clearly still in the deep stages of grief. "I really want to learn how to make cabinets," Micah offered.

"Daed's done that," Simon said, nudging his father.

"Done a little bit of everything," Lemuel said grudgingly.

"Do you get a lot of Englisch looking for that type of thing up here?" Micah asked.

"Not as many as you do down by Lancaster," Simon replied.

The foreman blew a whistle, the signal for them to get back to work. Micah drained the rest of his coffee, feeling more energized after Candace's amazing brownies.

"Where's your lunch pail?" Lemuel asked, closing the picnic basket and hefting it back up the stairs.

Micah ducked his head sheepishly. "I left it in the van. Lou says there's a doughnut shop down the road. I'll hurry there during our lunch break. Can I bring you back something when I go?"

Shaking his head, Lemuel said, "Nee. Don't go to the Englisch shops. We have enough."

"Like I said, Candace packed plenty," Simon said. "That is, if you like egg salad."

"There's a secret ingredient in that too," Gabriel piped up.

Micah hesitated. He was sure his cousins would provide for him if he tracked them down, but he didn't want to make their lunches less just because he had been careless. "If you're sure there is enough, I would be grateful for it. And you don't have to give away any more family secrets, Gabriel. I'm happy to be pleasantly surprised."

Simon clapped him on the shoulder. "There is more than enough. You will be doing us a favor by helping us eat all the food. Candace's feelings will be hurt if we don't, and I don't see how she expects us to eat as many sandwiches as she packed."

"Well, we can't have that. Not when she went through so much effort to bring it to you." Micah smiled again at the memory of her vaulting from the buggy and sliding on the ice to make her delivery. He couldn't imagine his sisters doing the same.

"I hope that stunt doesn't come back to haunt her," Lemuel said grimly.

"What do you mean?"

"She rode past the bishop's house. Might get a stern talking-to."

The man's voice was expressionless and his face was blank. Was he really talking about Candace?

It was true, Candace hadn't behaved with the calm consideration the Amish prized. Driving the buggy that fast over the snow could have caused an accident. Still, he hoped she didn't get in too much trouble for it. He thought it was admirable that she'd risked injury to make sure her family had a homemade meal.

"Why don't you stop by the farm on Saturday for lunch? You can tell Candace in person that you liked her brownies," Simon said.

"I'll check with my Aenti to make sure she doesn't have any plans for me." Micah was pretty sure Aenti Judy would be relieved at one less mouth to feed.

"I'll show you around my workshop," Lemuel said.

Simon did a double take at his father, then faced Micah again. "Yeah, please come over."

"All right."

Simon and Lemuel walked inside and veered to the left where they had been framing one of the rooms. Putting on his dust mask, Micah went back to hauling trash out to the dumpster. He wasn't building anything yet, but even so he enjoyed the hard work and the camaraderie of the other men.

And he'd just been invited to the Beacheys' home, which meant he'd get to see Candace again. That was a thing, he realized, that he wouldn't mind one bit.

3

Candace had made it on time for work—barely—and had just finished mixing up a batch of oatmeal raisin cookies when her boss, Karen, came up to her. They'd only been open an hour, but Karen already looked like she was at the end of her rope.

The Randolph Amish Market was a discount store known for its good prices, but also for selling Amish food and items. Many local Amish worked there as stockers and cashiers as well. Candace helped out in the bakery and sold some of her goat-milk lotions and soaps on consignment.

"I'll need you on a register this morning."

Inwardly, Candace groaned. She had been looking forward to doing her usual baking and maybe chatting with her friends Betsy or Mary while they worked. Still, this was her job and she needed it, so she'd do as she was told without complaining. "All right. I should have the next round of bread ready to rise in a few minutes. But I'll have to come back later to punch it down."

"Don't worry about it. Just take register four as soon as you're done with the bread and cookies, and we'll figure it out as we go."

"Okay."

Karen left without her usual chitchat and Candace was glad to have a moment to herself. She took her time—but not too much time—measuring out the flour, yeast, and water, then scooped in some lard and a few tablespoons of sugar and just a bit of salt. After she mixed all the ingredients together, Candace covered the bread dough with plastic wrap and set it aside. She then whipped up a huge batch of chocolate chip cookie dough, scooped out evenly sized portions, and placed them in the oven to bake while she made the molasses cookies.

Betsy came in just as Candace was switching trays in the oven, her brown eyes calm as usual below the wisps of honey-brown hair that peeked out from under her Kapp. She moved with such serenity and grace that Candace would have been jealous, if Betsy wasn't her best friend.

"Are we out of sheet pans?" Betsy asked, glancing around the kitchen.

"Ja, these are the last of them until you put the chocolate chip cookies on the cooling rack and wash off their pans."

Betsy hovered over the cookies that had just come out of the oven for a moment, clearly deliberating. "I'll get started on the rolls. I don't want to burn my fingers." She started making her dough and they worked side by side in silence while Candace made cinnamon sticky rolls.

"So," Betsy said after several minutes of silence, "are you going to tell me what all that was about this morning? You were driving that horse like your house was on fire."

"You're not going to believe it, but my Daed went to work today." Candace filled her in on the Pennsylvania carpentry job and why she had been rushing through the Millers' yard so early this morning.

"That's wonderful," Betsy said. "Will he attend the next church service?"

Candace bit her lip. "I'm sure he will." She wasn't sure of anything of the sort, but her father had never outright refused to go to church. He simply hadn't gotten out of bed in time. But it stood to reason that now he would. He had probably needed the time to grieve in his own way.

"Me too. I know my Daed and the deacons are worried."

"I was worried too, but I think everything is going to be all right."

It had to be. Candace took out the molasses cookies and put in the cinnamon rolls. She transferred the chocolate chip cookies onto the cookie rack, then washed and dried the sheet pans. "Aren't you going to tell me about Micah Zehr?"

"Oh." Betsy's shoulders sank. "Him."

Before Candace could ask her about her response, Karen poked her head into the kitchen. "Candace, I need you on register four." She disappeared again.

Sighing, Candace washed and dried her hands. "If I get held up, can you punch down the bread dough? And keep an eye on what's in the oven?"

"Ja, don't worry about it."

Candace was still curious about her friend's odd reaction to the mention of Micah, but she was being paid to work, not to talk to her friend. Hopefully, they could take a break or lunch together—*oh no.* She had been so busy making her family's lunch that she'd forgotten to make her own. Shaking her head, Candace signed out the register drawer from the security station and went to set it up in register four. Now she would have to give up her morning break to go shopping.

It was a busy few hours, and before she knew it, Karen signaled to her to shut off her light and take her fifteen minutes. She grabbed a basket and hurried to get the things she knew she would need for tonight. As she tossed blueberries, snacks, and lunch meat into her cart, she couldn't help but feel a pang of homesickness. She wished she was home, with a beef stew cooking in the kitchen. Then she could take a real break with her knitting or a book. That would have to wait until Saturday or Sunday, though.

"Candace Beachey, how are you?"

"*Guder Mariye*, Emma." She glanced at the clock on the wall. "I'm sorry, I can't chat. I'm on my break, and I need to finish some shopping."

Emma Scwhartz nodded and looked a bit disappointed. "Do you know if you have any more of these green beans in the back?"

"I don't. But I can see if I can find someone to help you."

"How's your Daed doing?"

"Great," Candace said, backing away. "He and Simon are on a jobsite together."

"*Gut.* I hope to see him in church next time."

You and me both.

Candace was able to check out and run her purchases back to her locker behind the bakery just before her break ended. "How's everything?" she asked Betsy, trying to catch her breath.

"Busy. I think we're going to run out of bread again."

Candace grimaced. Karen hated when that happened.

"I haven't even had time to make the pies, even though the crusts are ready," Betsy said.

"Excuse me, Miss? Can I get this pan of sticky buns and four molasses cookies?"

"Ja, of course," Betsy said. She turned to Candace and said quietly in *Deistsch*, "I haven't had my break yet. After this customer, can you watch the bakery for fifteen minutes?"

"Sure. Karen's up front. I'll even see if I can get the pies in the oven."

"Denki." Betsy turned back to the customer.

As Candace pressed the piecrusts into the disposable pie tins, she thought that maybe when she got married—not that there was anyone special in her life now—she could work part-time instead of full-time. Candace would find this job a lot more fulfilling if she could make pies for her family instead of for strangers. She got an assembly line going and had all the crusts in the pans in record time. Grabbing some mason jars of pie fillings from the store's big refrigerator, she balanced six of them and brought them out to the large worktable.

She dumped peach filling into one piecrust, apple filling into another, and blueberry into the third. Rhubarb, lemon, and strawberry fillings went into the other three. Then Candace placed a top piecrust on each one and fluted the edges by pinching them deftly between her fingers. She wished there was time to add more decoration. There were a few jars of cherry pie filling in the fridge and she had been wanting to try a lattice crust she'd seen in a magazine. But they needed these out as quickly as possible.

One thing she did like about baking in the store was the large oven. She was able to fit all the pies in there at once. Dusting off her hands then setting the timer, Candace took a look at what needed to be replenished. The display case held slim pickings. They needed to do another batch of cookies and the basket of rolls was almost empty as well.

"Candace to the front," came a voice over the loudspeaker.

She hid her groan and hoped that Betsy had heard the announcement and wouldn't think she'd abandoned her. There were lines winding their way out of each register. She wasn't sure what was going on, but they were sure busy. Candace didn't like this fast pace. It made her nervous and when she got nervous, she made mistakes.

By midafternoon, Candace was ready to curl up for a nap. But instead, she went back to the bakery and into their small break room that doubled as a walk-in pantry. Famished, she made herself a ham-and-cheese sandwich and opened a bag of chips. Sitting at the small table, she bowed her head in a quick prayer. *Another meal alone.*

As she was finishing up her lunch, Betsy came in and flopped down in the plastic seat across from her.

"They're calling for snow tomorrow," she said, pulling out her own lunch.

Candace tried not to be jealous of Betsy's leftover fried chicken and macaroni and cheese, and instead drank some bottled iced tea that was a shade sweeter than how she normally made it. Capping it, she put the rest of it in the fridge for later.

"Well, that explains the frenzy." Candace wasn't used to feeling so tired, and she propped her head up with her hand as she slumped on the table.

"Are you okay?"

"I'm not sure. I feel weepy, stressed, and all out of sorts."

"I think it's your body's reaction to this morning. My father is planning to speak with your father."

Wincing, Candace straightened up. "About my driving?"

"More about that he needs to come to church. But yeah, you driving like a maniac will probably come up as well."

Candace nodded. "It couldn't be helped. I'm set for the rest of the week." She pointed at her groceries. "I'll do some more cooking this weekend to be better prepared."

"It will be fine. Especially if Lemuel returns to his chores and tends to the animals."

"That would be nice." She was worried about her father and wondered how he was faring on the jobsite. He was probably going to be hungry tonight, and if Esther was feeling poorly, Candace should invite her brother's family to supper as well. She could pick up a rotisserie chicken and some noodles and make a brown butter sauce. If she hid the plastic container, Daed might not notice it wasn't homemade. Or if she dug out the stove-top waffle maker, she could make chicken with waffles and then do some extra to have breakfast already prepared.

"Candace, are you even listening to me?" Betsy demanded.

"Nee, I'm sorry. My mind is wandering. What were you saying?"

"I was telling you all about Micah Zehr. Why did you ask about him earlier?"

That made her sit up straighter. "I met him this morning. Well, I ran into him. Literally." Candace explained that part of the story, which she had left out before.

"You think he's handsome?" Betsy said with disbelief.

"You don't?" Candace matched her tone.

"He's all right, I guess. I think Amos Eicher is a better example of handsome."

"Amos." Candace made a face.

"What's wrong with Amos?" Betsy sounded indignant.

"His Mamm says he's going to ask me to step out with him in the spring."

"Oh." Betsy's eyes lowered and she played with the hem of her apron.

"Have you met Micah yet? I think there's matchmaking afoot there," she teased.

"Maybe." Betsy sighed. "Yes, probably. My father and his father met at my sister's wedding last year. Micah's father is a minister, and I think he might be a candidate for their next bishop. It's a *gut* match. *Daed* says Micah will get farmland when he marries. It's a prosperous area." Betsy sounded like she was trying to convince herself.

"Prosperous?" Candace raised an eyebrow. "Then why is he working with my father and brother at a job hours away?"

"I don't know. Maybe Daed just wants me married and out of his house. Lately, it doesn't seem like I can do anything right." Betsy picked at her lunch.

"All fathers want their daughters to be happily married. Micah seems like the perfect candidate," Candace said lightly. *Too perfect to be true.*

"You're probably right, but I don't see why my father would prefer him over someone local."

"You have to admit," Candace said with a small smile, "it sounds very romantic. A handsome stranger coming to town and sweeping you off your feet."

"Candace to the front."

This time, Candace did groan. "I'd much rather be back here baking with you."

"Have you seen the work that's piling up out there?" Betsy said. "I'd much rather be in my own home."

Candace knew how she felt. "Trina should be here soon to help you out." She stood and put her perishable food in the walk-in cooler and the rest in her locker.

"If I last that long. At least if I get married and move to Pennsylvania, I'll be too busy working at home to consider a job in a store."

Candace pushed away envious thoughts. "I would miss you if you go."

"I haven't left yet."

Candace forced a bright smile on her face. "You're right. No sense thinking about that now." She hated that they could never finish a conversation at work. It was always rush, rush, rush. It would have been so nice if they were at home, either Candace's or Betsy's, with a pot of tea and a slice of pie. But that would have to wait until the weather was nicer and they could both get a day off at the same time, or after church.

As she made her way back up to the register, Candace tried not to think about the rest of the afternoon. Her thoughts turned to her goats, who always made her happy. Actually, they made anyone who watched them happy. Her Englisch neighbor Krystal adored them. She wanted to borrow them for something she called "goat yoga."

During the warm summer months, Krystal held yoga classes outside on her beautifully manicured lawn. Candace thought if she let her goats loose, they would eat all of Krystal's flowers, but Krystal said she didn't care. She wanted to put them in children's pajamas and have them prance around her exercising clients. Mamm had thought it a ridiculous idea, but Candace thought it might work out—if she could figure out a way to get them to Krystal's studio and back.

Candace could almost hear her Mamm's voice. *Who would sign up to have goats jump on them when they exercise? No one, that's who.*

She would give anything to be able to argue with her mother about it again.

Candace had recently seen an article in one of the magazines by her checkout register on dwarf goat yoga and wished she could have shown her mother that it really was something Englisch people did, silly as it seemed. Maybe Krystal would let her have a small farm stand to sell her goat-milk lotion, soap, and body cream to the yoga clients. Or maybe she could open her own shop and ask Krystal to send her clients over. She could set up an adjacent petting zoo with the goats. These were lovely thoughts. She only hoped they were enough to keep her motivated as she worked.

Candace unlocked her cash register drawer. Turning on her overhead light, she forced a smile and beckoned a customer over. As she rang up the purchases, she wondered about marriage. If Amos Eicher did ask Candace to step out and they wound up married, her life wouldn't change much at all. Maybe they would get a small piece of farmland to build their house on, but it was more likely Amos would move in with her and Daed.

But if Betsy married Micah, she would leave, and then Candace wouldn't have her friend to talk to at work, no matter how briefly. It didn't seem fair that after losing her Mamm, Candace might lose Betsy too.

Things had been so different when Mamm was alive. These past three months had seemed like three years. Back then Candace had only been working part-time at the store and the rest of her day was spent taking care of their home and family. She and her Mamm had had a system. While her Daed was on a job or working in his woodshop, they would cook first, then clean, and then spend some time reading or sewing until lunch. Then, if they were all caught up on chores, they would go visiting and help their neighbors or work in the gardens until supper. Daed would be smiling when he came in, and her mother would sing hymns in the house.

But now the house was quiet all the time, and Daed never smiled.

"Are you all right?" a young Englisch mother asked her.

Candace was startled and then realized her face was all wet. She wiped away tears she hadn't known she was shedding and said, "Ja, I must be allergic to something."

The woman nodded understandingly and helped bag her own groceries while her Kinner sat in the grocery cart. Candace made it a point to smile at them.

The next customer was Mary Stoltzfus and she wasn't fooled by the allergies remark. "You've been under a lot of pressure since your Mamm died," she said, placing her canned goods and big boxes of cereal on the conveyer belt.

"I'm fine, Mary."

"People who are fine don't cry without realizing it. You need to take some time off."

She couldn't afford to, but she wasn't going to admit it. "I will," she said instead. "Thank you for worrying about me. Aren't you working today?"

"I'm on break. I figured I'd get some shopping done."

Candace nodded. "Ja, I did that too. Do you have a coupon for the cereal? I think I saw one in the flyer."

"Nee." Mary frowned.

Shuffling around under the register, Candace found a copy. "Got one."

"Denki."

Candace smiled and nodded and started ringing up the next customer. A vacation would be nice. Maybe she could go visit her sister in Pinecraft, Florida. But that would be a long train ride. It might be worth it to get out of the weather, but with Esther due so soon she couldn't leave, and by the time everything settled with that, it would be springtime. Candace just needed to hang in there a little bit more until then. Spring would be a fresh beginning for everyone.

Her father included, she hoped.

4

The promised snowstorm dumped another foot of snow on them, and the plows weren't done with the roads in time for the van to pick up any of the other Amish workers in the area. Micah worried about getting in trouble, but the bishop stopped by to let them know the Mennonite company understood that it would be unsafe for them to travel when the roads weren't plowed. Micah and his cousins had plenty of work to do shoveling their own yard so they would be ready to go tomorrow when the plows cleared the roads.

"I'm so sick of snow," Amos complained.

"Ja, and in August you're going to be caterwauling about the heat," his brother John said with a grin.

"Less talking, more shoveling. The quicker we do this, the quicker we can go inside and relax." The youngest Eicher brother, Arnie, kept his head down and his snow shovel moving.

Micah smiled at the brotherly banter, missing his own brothers back in Pennsylvania. They would probably be doing the same thing right now, depending on how much snow they got. His older brother, Benjamin, would probably use the farm tractor, which had the steel wheels allowed by their bishop, to push the snow to one side into great big banks that his Kinner would then climb all over.

It was lunchtime when they finished clearing the paths to the driveway and the barn.

While his cousins decided to take an afternoon nap by the

woodstove, Micah was restless. Aenti Judy looked up from her sewing. "You look like you're brimming with energy."

"I wish we could go to work now that the roads are clearer."

Judy snorted. "By the time you got there, it'd be time to come home."

"Do you mind if I hook up the sleigh and go visit Lemuel Beachey?"

"Lemuel?" she said in surprise. "Why?"

"He and I were talking yesterday, and he and Simon invited me to see his woodshop. Unless you need me?"

"Nee, but you work too hard. You should rest."

"If I rest now, I'll never get to sleep tonight."

"How did Lemuel seem to you?" she asked, setting her mending aside.

"He was quiet. Why?"

"Yesterday was the first time anyone has seen him since his wife died during the harvest last year. He has barely left his house or even his bedroom in almost three months."

Micah frowned. "He did seem sad, but he worked hard and shared his lunch with me when I forgot mine in the van."

"He always was a kind man. I'm glad he's coming out of the darkness, but I should warn you. There have been rumors about him." She stopped rocking in her chair and gestured for him to sit across from her.

Micah did, but he said, "I don't listen to gossip."

"It's not gossip. It's the truth. He hasn't been to church since Sarah's funeral."

"Has he been ill? Have the roads been impassable for sleighs on those Sundays?" It usually took something very serious to keep an Amish man from worship. Micah was trying to search for a reason that made sense and he was coming up empty. The sleds worked fine in deep snow, and unless he had been in the hospital, there wasn't any reason that Lemuel should have missed church.

"Nee, unless you count being heartsick as a debilitating illness. When I lost your *Onkel* John, I was devastated. But I had three boys to take care of. Lemuel is lucky his children are adults and are taking care of him. I never missed a day of church in my life. I needed it even more after John's passing. The rumors are that Lemuel has lost his faith."

That concerned him greatly. No Amish man should be without the comfort of Gött and His words of hope. Micah stood up. "Has anyone asked him?"

"He wouldn't come downstairs for any guests who visited. You will be the first that he's shown an interest in. I wanted you to understand about him. Maybe your visiting will help."

Taking her hands in his, he said, "I will do everything in my power to help him, but we're going to build things, not have a heart-to-heart." Micah found that people tuned out lectures, no matter how well meaning. While they were doing something they both loved, however, perhaps Micah could start a conversation that would help Lemuel find his way back to Gött, if he had indeed left Him.

Judy smiled and patted his cheek. "Go then. But don't go empty-handed. Take a loaf of banana bread over with you."

Micah did, and he also snagged one of the jars of strawberry jam that his mother had sent from home. He thought it would be a nice a thank-you present for Candace for packing extra sandwiches yesterday.

"Do you even know how to get there?" Judy asked.

"I guess I don't," he said sheepishly.

She gave him simple directions. Their farm wasn't that far away. In better weather, it would be walkable. It wasn't the same route that Candace had used, given the direction she'd come from, but that was probably because the back fields she'd taken would no doubt still be unplowed. After he hitched up the horse to the sleigh, he was glad to be out in the fresh air. His aunt's house was cramped and he missed his family. As he drove through the snow, he pretended he was back home, at least for a little while.

While shoveling wasn't his favorite activity, the absolute quiet after a heavy snowfall was enchanting. He wished he had someone to share it with. It didn't take long for him to arrive at the Beachey house. The drive hadn't yet been shoveled. Hopping down from the sleigh, he was glad for his warm boots as he trudged to the front door.

He knocked and waited, wishing he had brought a snow shovel. He could have helped clear off the porch and stairs. Candace opened the door with a quizzical look on her face.

"Micah?" Her expression of surprise quickly turned welcoming.

He broke out into a wide grin. She knew his name. "Lemuel invited me to come over sometime and see his workshop. I figured today was a good day as any."

He was fascinated by the range of emotions that flashed over her face.

"It actually isn't a good day, but please come in and get warm. Would you like some coffee or tea?"

"That would be nice. Here." He held out the gifts he'd brought. "Aenti Judy sent her banana bread and my Mamm made the jam."

Candace led him into the dining room. He noticed it was a bit colder in the house than he was used to. But the house smelled wonderful with aromas of chicken noodle soup and fresh-baked bread wrapping around him.

"I wanted to thank you for packing extra sandwiches yesterday. I had left my lunch in the van and your family was gracious enough to share with me. It was delicious."

"I'm so glad you enjoyed it. Did they leave you any brownies?"

"I can't ever remember having better ones—don't tell my Mamm."

Giggling, Candace hid her face. "You're kind to say so." She wrapped her shawl around her tighter and looked away.

"Would you like me to light the woodstove?" he asked, feeling the chill through his coat.

"Oh." Her face twisted in dismay. "I've been in the kitchen all day. I haven't brought in any wood from the shed."

"I'll go." Micah buttoned his coat again.

She blushed a deep red. "I-I'm afraid it's not shoveled. You'll get your pant legs all wet."

"Where's your shovel?"

"You don't have to do that," she protested.

"I don't mind, especially if there's a bowl of that soup and a wedge of bread waiting for me after."

She gave him a grateful smile. "Of course. It'll be here whether you shovel or not."

"I'll be back soon." He paused in the doorway. "If you don't mind me asking, where's your Daed?"

She froze in place, her mouth pressing together. "Um . . . he's not feeling well. I'm going to take him some soup now."

Micah nodded. "Please tell him I hope he feels better and not to worry about the snow. I'll take care of it."

"Denki," she whispered and turned away, but not before he saw a shimmer of tears in her eyes.

Grabbing the shovel from the back porch, he cleared a path to the woodshed. Micah noticed that there were deep boot prints going to and from the barn. Candace must have trudged out there to feed the animals. Setting the shovel up by the door, Micah gathered an armful of logs from the shed and brought them back to the house.

Doing his best not to track a lot of snow in the house, he set the wood down by the large stove, then selected a few of the correct size to load into the chamber. After lighting the stove, he looked around for Candace, but she wasn't there. *Upstairs with her Daed*, he figured.

Micah brought in two more loads of logs and set them up by the stove. That should last her until tomorrow.

Going back out, he dug a path to the barn and checked on the animals. They had fresh food and water. The little goats were bleating and prancing, and he wished he knew what they wanted. They didn't seem cold, so he added more hay to their feed tray.

As he was walking back to the house, he heard a whistle from the next farm over. Squinting, he thought he recognized Simon's coat. He waved. Simon brandished a snow shovel and gestured to the house. Not entirely sure what he meant, Micah went back inside. Candace bustled around the kitchen. He noticed that she had put on a different dress and had straightened her Kapp. Why had she done that? Micah thought she was beautiful just the way she had been.

"Are you ready for that soup now?" she asked.

"Is that Simon's farm next door?"

"It is. Was he out there?"

"Ja, I think he wants some help shoveling and now that I'm warmed up, I'll go give him a hand. How's your Daed?"

Her smile flickered. "He's eating. Thank you for getting the wood. What's your favorite cookie? I'll make a batch while you're out there with Simon."

Micah was sure anything she made would be his favorite. "Surprise me."

A few minutes later, Micah was back outside and working. Simon was shoveling toward him with Gabriel helping. Micah hefted the snow away from the house and turned to make a connecting path with Simon. It took a good hour, but they met in the middle and paused to catch their breath.

"It's good to see you," Simon said. "Is everything all right?"

"Ja, I had come to visit with your father, but he's not feeling well."

Simon sighed. "I was afraid of that. How's Candace?"

"*Gut*. She was baking and made some soup for him. She said he was eating."

Nodding, Simon walked with him back to the house. "Feel up to helping me with Daed's driveway?"

"Sure." Together, the three of them finished the driveway quickly and had a brief snowball fight before heading inside. This time, the house felt warm and welcoming in addition to the wonderful cooking smells. He hung up his coat by Simon's and kicked off his boots.

"I hope you worked up an appetite," Candace called out.

The dining room table was set up for them with large soup bowls and a basket of sliced bread that steamed lightly. They each drained their glasses of iced tea before even sitting down. Shoveling was thirsty work.

"I'm starving," Gabriel said, clutching his stomach dramatically. "I haven't had anything since breakfast."

"Which was only a few hours ago," Simon said, chuckling.

"He's a growing boy," Candace said protectively. "Now, sit down and we'll have something to eat." She refilled their glasses and went back into the kitchen.

Candace came back staggering under the weight of a huge pot. Micah jumped up to help her carry it to the table and set it down. Ladling them each out a large portion of soup, Candace went back into the kitchen. It was a thick soup with chunks of chicken, vegetables, and wide strips of noodles. His stomach growled in anticipation, even though he'd also had a big breakfast a few hours ago. His aunt had made stacks of pancakes, and they'd used up the last of the maple syrup. His cousins remarked that it was a good thing the sap would be flowing soon so they could make more.

Candace returned with a crock of butter and something else.

"Candace makes her own butter and goat cheese," Simon explained.

"I can't wait to try it."

Simon led them in a quick prayer and they got down to eating. It was silent for the first few minutes as everyone dug in. The soup tasted as good as it smelled, and he said as much to Candace.

"Denki. I like making something hearty on a day like this." She beamed at him, her clear blue eyes sparkling.

Micah was glad he was sitting down.

"You should try her chili," Simon said.

"I like her pizza," Gabriel said. "We haven't had that in a long time."

Candace cocked her head. "You know, you're right. I should make some for supper this week. How about on Friday? Micah can come home with you from work and I'll have it all ready."

"With soda?" Gabriel asked.

"I think I can arrange that," she said. "I work at the Randolph Amish Market in town." she explained to Micah. "Normally, I work in the bakery with—" She broke off, coughing.

"I hope you're not getting sick," Micah said.

She waved him off. "I can't get sick. I've got too much to do." She stood up and brought in another pitcher of iced tea and refilled all their glasses again.

"How do you like working at the store?"

"It depends on the day." Candace sighed. "I like that it's steady work. Rain or shine, all year long. I love baking, so when I get to spend the day just doing that, it's almost like being home. But sometimes I have to fill in at the checkout counters up front, and I don't like that as much." She shrugged. "What about your new job? Is it similar to what you did back home?"

"Nee. I have a small woodshop that I tinker in back home. My Daed thinks it's a waste of time because there are fields to prepare, plant, pick, or plow, but I like making and building things. Eventually,

I'd like to set up a cabinet shop. I've still got a lot to learn before I can do that, though."

He looked into her eyes a bit too long. It made him feel light-headed, and her smile made heat creep into his face.

"My Daed built all of our upstairs furniture," Candace said, breaking eye contact. He noticed her cheeks were also a pretty pink. "Not to mention this table and chairs."

"Really?" Micah was impressed. The table and chairs were solid and sturdy, with fine craftsmanship.

"He wanted to open up his own store too, instead of always working for other people. That's probably why he took such a shine to you when you mentioned that was your interest as well," Simon said, spreading goat cheese on a thick slice of bread.

"I'm happy about that," Candace said, favoring him with another sweet smile. "He hasn't been interested in anything since Mamm passed."

Micah ducked his head in embarrassment. He wasn't anything special, but he was glad to play some small part in helping Lemuel with his grief. "I didn't see a workshop outside when I was shoveling," Micah said.

"It's behind the barn."

"Let's shovel back out to there." Micah pushed back from the table.

Simon and Candace exchanged a look. "That won't be necessary," she said.

"It's not a problem at all," Micah said. "Besides, it will help us earn those cookies. What kind did you make?"

She ducked her head. "I made a yellow cake instead. It's my Mamm's recipe. And it seemed more festive than cookies."

Gabriel pumped his fist. "Yes! What kind of frosting?"

"Chocolate buttercream."

"Let's go!" Gabriel ran from the table to get on his coat.

"Maybe afterward, we can play a board game?" Candace suggested.

"I'd like that," Micah said. His aunt might get to wondering when he was coming back, but she did say she wanted him to rest and relax. He couldn't think of a nicer way to do that than eating cake and playing a game with Candace and her family.

5

The next morning the roads were clear enough for the van to get through and everybody was scheduled to go back to work. Candace padded to her father's door and knocked on it.

"Daed?" she called out. "The van will be here in an hour."

She didn't expect an answer, and she didn't get one. It was so discouraging. She had thought that they were out of the woods when he went to work on Monday. But the snowstorm seemed to have thrown him, and he'd gone back to bed and more or less stayed there.

Micah had been a blessing when he'd come over and helped. In addition to the work he'd done, he'd filled the house with fun and laughter again. At least for a little while. After everyone had gone home, the dreariness had set back in. But since she only had her own chores to do, she could clean the house and do a load of laundry. It was currently hanging in her bedroom with the woodstove burning on high to take away the damp and stiffness of the clothes. Looking at the calendar, Candace's shoulders slumped. They still had a long way to go until spring.

She headed out to the barn and did her father's morning chores. Digging out the goats' play area again, she wished she could be home at noon to let them out to romp for a while during the warmest part of the day.

When she came back inside, she packed them both a thermos of chicken noodle soup and a bologna-and-cheese sandwich. But Candace didn't have the heart or the inclination to make breakfast. Not if it was just going to be her. She plodded up the stairs to her father's room again.

"Daed? I'm going over to Simon's before work. Your lunch is on the table. The van will be at Simon's in about half an hour. I'll see you tonight."

No answer.

Candace shrugged. She had done all she could. Hooking Belle up to the buggy, she drove the short distance to Simon's house. She could hear Gabriel and baby Abraham chattering away and Esther singing in the kitchen. Pausing in the doorway, she let the happy sounds of the household fill her. This was what she wanted for herself, for her father, for all of them. Letting herself in, she unwrapped her scarf and hung up her coat.

"Aenti Candace!" Gabriel called.

Little Abraham toddled toward her, making delighted squeals, and she caught him just before he fell over. Hoisting him on her hip, she joined Simon and Esther at the dining room table.

"How are you feeling?" she asked her sister-in-law, setting Abraham in his high chair.

"Better than yesterday. Thank you for sending over the ginger tea. It really helped. There's some leftover hash and eggs if you're hungry."

"Denki, I'll have some." Candace toasted some bread and made herself a plate. Part of her felt a pang of guilt that her father didn't have breakfast. But he also hadn't come down or answered her knocks.

"How's Daed?" Simon asked quietly when she sat down at the table with her breakfast.

She shook her head, and Simon sighed, rubbing his forehead. "Esther, can you check up on Daed around noon?" he asked.

"Ja, Abraham and I will go over and see if we can coax him to come home with us until you come back from work."

"Thank you," Candace said. "And if it's not too much trouble, can you let the goats out for a couple of hours if it warms up?"

Esther smiled. "Sure. Abraham loves to watch them."

"So do I." She should put some of their milk to good use and make some more soaps and lotions. They were running low at the store. Maybe she could tackle that tonight if she felt up to it.

"Are the animals all taken care of, or do you need help to do it?" Simon asked.

"I took care of them this morning." After saying a quick prayer, she dug into her breakfast. It always tasted better when someone else made it, and Esther was an excellent cook. Candace smiled at her gratefully when she set a cup of coffee in front of her.

"What's going to happen with your Daed at the job? Will he be fired?" Esther fretted.

"Not yet. The foreman might ask where he is, and I'll say he's sick."

"That's not *gut*," Esther said.

"If he decides not to go back, maybe we can find someone else to take his place," Candace suggested. "Do you think any of our Englisch neighbors are looking for work?"

Simon shook his head. "There's no one that I know of. We'll pick up the slack, though. He was an extra hand to begin with."

The van beeped its horn outside, and the fragment of hope that Candace had been clinging to shattered. Her father hadn't gotten up to go to work. They were right back where they'd started. And she didn't know what to do.

"I'll see you all tonight," Simon said as he stood.

"Are you sure I can't come with you, Daed?" Gabriel asked.

"Not today, Gabriel. You still need to go to school, and you better start walking now or you'll be late."

"Okay," Gabriel grumbled and followed his father out, swinging his lunch pail.

"I should be going too," Candace said, but her heart wasn't in it.

It wasn't that she couldn't understand why her father didn't want to get out of bed this morning, or why the snow yesterday had set him back. Some days, she also wished she could bury herself under the covers and dream of better times.

"Can you stay for a bit?" Esther asked. "It gets a little lonely this time of year with just the baby to keep me company. Although I'm not going to be able to call him my baby any longer in a few weeks."

"I've got a few minutes." Candace helped Abraham down from his chair, while Esther took their coffee into the living room. They sat on the couch and watched Abraham play with a wooden toy. It would be so nice to stay here all day. And if she'd had her knitting with her, she could work on the baby blanket that she was making for the new Boppli. She had wanted to finish it by Christmas, but the timing hadn't worked out.

"Before you know it, he'll be going off to school."

"I know and I'll miss him when he's gone." Esther put her swollen feet up on the ottoman. "But I'll be glad for the peace and quiet."

"You wouldn't if that was all you had," Candace said, trying to keep the bitterness out of her voice.

"Why don't you and Daed come and stay here for a little while?" Esther suggested kindly. "We have plenty of room."

Candace shook her head. "You're going to have your hands full with the new Boppli, and Daed won't budge."

"You deserve some time to yourself," Esther insisted. "When was the last time you made soaps?"

"It's been a while," she admitted. "I've just been so tired when I get home. And I know it's not fair to rely on Simon to help out every day. But he's made things easier."

Esther shrugged. "That's what family is for. Does Daed need anything?"

"He shouldn't. If he does come downstairs, there are blueberry muffins and some coffee you can heat up for him. His lunch is on the counter, and I made a meat loaf for supper tonight. He's got wood for the stove in his bedroom. He should be fine."

"I'll take care of it. You can enjoy work without worrying about him."

Candace gave her a small smile. "If they keep me back in the bakery with Mary, it should be a good day." Today was Betsy's day off. Candace's day off this week was Friday. She was planning on doing a thorough house cleaning while the pizza dough rose. That was something to look forward to. She felt her spirits lifting. "Do you want me to bring you back anything from the store?"

"I've been craving a cherry pie."

"If I get time to make one, it's all yours."

"Thanks," she said. "So, tell me about Micah Zehr. It looked like he was your knight in shining snow shovel yesterday."

"He was." Candace grinned, thinking about it. "I had such a nice day yesterday, all things considered. I was upset because Daed wouldn't get out of bed, but when Micah showed up, it felt like everything would be all right."

"It sounds like you'd accept if he asked you to step out."

Candace shook her head. "I can't think about that right now."

"Why not?"

"Well, for one thing, Bishop Mark wants him to marry Betsy."

"It's not the bishop's decision," Esther pointed out. "What does Betsy think?"

"From the little we talked about it, she didn't seem too keen on the idea. But her father thinks it's a good match. And Judy Eicher says Amos is going to ask me to step out."

"*Gut*," Esther said. "I hope he does, and you can all have some fun. I'll see if I can put a bug in Simon's ear to host a skating frolic this weekend. We can invite the whole community and have a get-together. I think we're all getting a little stir-crazy with this weather."

A tickle of excitement stirred in Candace's stomach. "That would be nice." Then she glanced at the clock. "I have to go. Thanks for breakfast and the chat."

"Anytime."

Feeling a little bit happier than she had earlier, Candace drove to work. Until she put on her apron at the market, it didn't occur to her that she hadn't checked on her father again like she usually did. A shock of panic raced through her, but she reminded herself that Esther would check on him in a few hours. It would be fine.

The morning was busy, but in a good way. The customers were back to normal, and she and Mary could concentrate on the baking. At lunchtime, Candace went outside and sat in the buggy because the weather was mild for a winter day. She wondered if her father had come downstairs yet. She hoped he was watching her goats with his grandson and enjoying his family

Her thoughts turned to Micah, as they seemed to be doing frequently now. She should do something nice for him to thank him for shoveling their snow yesterday. Since she was already planning to make a cherry pie for Esther, a second one for Micah would be just the thing.

She managed to make three pies from the filling they had in stock and told Mary she was going to box up two of them to buy once they were done.

"Make a few apple and a mixed-berry one while you're at it," Mary said. She was scooping out snickerdoodle cookies to bake.

They worked together in companionable silence that was broken up by the occasional customer. The breads were selling steadily, but Candace didn't want to make too many loaves. Although, the day-old loaves were great in her father's coffee soup.

Again, she wondered how he was doing.

A few hours before her shift ended, Candace and Mary were bagging rolls when Esther came into the bakery with Gabriel and Abraham in tow.

"I would have brought back the cherry pie," Candace said, her voice trailing off when she saw Esther's face. "What's wrong?" she whispered.

Mary must have picked up on the tension in their faces. "I think I have a few broken cookies in back that I can't sell. Why don't you boys come with me?" She took the two boys into the break room.

"The bishop showed up at the house while we were letting the goats out," Esther said.

Her heart sped up. "What did you tell him?"

"I said that Lemuel wasn't feeling well and wasn't up for visitors."

Candace put her hand over her heart. "Denki."

"Don't thank me. He went upstairs anyway."

"What?" Candace's mind raced. Thankfully, she had cleaned her Daed's room on Monday while she was waiting for him to come home. She hoped the bishop wouldn't go into her room and see the clean clothes still hanging there, not put away. Had she left dishes in the sink? "I should go home. I'll have to cut my shift short."

"Don't," Esther said. "The bishop's gone. I stayed and made some tea, but when the bishop came back down, he didn't want any."

"Did he say anything else?" Candace hugged herself tight, feeling a chill of apprehension spread through her.

Esther shook her head. "He just told me to have a nice day. I went upstairs to ask what happened, and Lemuel told me not to worry myself and to go home."

"Did he eat?"

"I brought him up a sandwich, but later he wouldn't let me in to take the tray back down."

Candace sighed. "I'm sorry he was so difficult. What do you think the bishop said?"

"I don't know. Is Betsy here?"

"Nee. It's her day off. We're working together tomorrow, so I'll see if I can get more information if Daed's still not talking tonight."

"Okay. I'm going to do some shopping while I'm here. If you find out anything tonight, stop over and let me know."

"I will."

Candace went back to work with her head reeling. When Mary came out to join her, Candace filled her in.

"Have you ever thought about taking him to the doctor?" Mary asked, checking the oven's timer.

"There's nothing physically wrong with him."

"Physically no. But there are medications that could help him over his depression and grief."

Candace thought about it. "I don't think I could get him to go. And we don't have the time or the money to waste on a doctor's trip anyway."

"Maybe that's something you could talk to the bishop about. If Lemuel won't see a doctor for you, perhaps the bishop could get him to go."

Candace caught Mary's sleeve. "Mary, he would have told us if he shunned my Daed, right?"

Mary nodded. "He would, and you know that's a last resort."

"I know. I'm just afraid I'm going to lose him too."

Mary put her hand on Candace's arm. "Why don't you take a break? Splash some water on your face and have some tea. I'll cover for you here."

"Denki." That sounded like a good idea. Taking a deep breath, she went in the back and poured herself some ginger tea from her thermos. Her stomach hadn't been doing so well lately either. She placed a hand over it. It would have been worth the gurgles if there were a Boppli in there, but that wasn't going to happen anytime soon. But that was just as well. Her Daed needed her, although she had no idea how to help him.

Betsy bustled in a few minutes later. Candace had just started to relax when her nerves frayed again at the sight of the bishop's daughter.

"It's okay," Betsy said, heading off her questions.

Candace slumped in her chair. "Oh, I'm so glad. What did your father want with my Daed?"

"He was concerned when Lemuel didn't go to work today."

"How did he find out so fast?"

"The foreman called the Mennonite company to complain. So, my Daed went to visit your Daed. He told him that he had mourned long enough and was putting too much of a burden on you and Simon."

Candace winced. "He shouldn't have said that."

"It's the truth and you know it."

"It seems so harsh to say it like that."

"Maybe, but it's my Daed's nature to speak frankly. Daed told Lemuel that he expected him to be at work every day because if he was going to keep not showing up, it was going to reflect badly on the community and that would affect future jobs coming in from the Mennonite company."

"How do you know all of this?"

"I overheard him talking to Judy Eicher when she came to visit this afternoon."

"Why was he telling Judy about my Daed?" Candace felt the first simmering of anger. It wasn't anyone's business what troubles her father was going through.

"Just wait. I'm not done with my story."

Candace was glad she was sitting down. Had the bishop warned Daed that he was in danger of being shunned for not going to church in so long?

"Judy had come over to visit with my Mamm. She happened to mention that Micah had gone to see Lemuel's workshop. My Daed thought it would be a good idea for Lemuel to take on Micah as an apprentice woodworker in their spare time."

An apprentice? Whatever Candace had expected Betsy to say, that had not been it.

Betsy eyed her sagely. "I think that between your Daed doing his chores again, going to work, and teaching Micah, he's not going to have time to stay in bed and mourn."

"That workshop hasn't been touched since before Mamm died." Candace hadn't had time to clean in there with all her other chores. Although, if her father was going to take on caring for their animals again, maybe now she would.

"He's sending Micah over on Saturday to help him get organized."

Candace couldn't tell if she felt better, more anxious, excited to see Micah again, or some combination of the three. "Did he say how my Daed took all of that?" Her father was so stubborn, she worried that he had given Bishop Mark an argument.

"He didn't say, but I think this is a positive thing."

Candace slowly nodded. "It might just be." She didn't dare count on it, but she felt a glimmer of hope. "Your Daed didn't mention missing church?"

"If he did, he didn't say anything about it to Judy. But I imagine it goes without saying that Lemuel will be in church a week from Sunday. Oh, and there was one more thing."

It figured. "I'm not sure I can take one more thing."

Betsy smirked at her. "Daed also said to tell you that just because Belle is retired from harness racing at Yonkers doesn't mean you should drive like you're on the track."

6

Micah was happy to see Lemuel back at work the next day. He was sullen and quiet, but Micah just assumed he was still getting over his cold, not that he appeared sick. He didn't get a chance to talk to the older man because they were on opposite ends of the building and had different break schedules.

At lunchtime, Simon motioned Micah over to eat with him.

"Everything all right?" Micah asked. "Your Daed seemed tired this morning."

"He's fine." Simon unwrapped a tuna salad sandwich.

Micah had a cold-cut sandwich and a corn muffin with some of his mother's jam on it. It was messy, but it tasted like home. He offered Simon one of Aenti Judy's oatmeal raisin cookies and took one of Esther's chocolate chip ones in return.

"Do you have any plans for Sunday?" Simon asked as he opened a bottle of orange soda.

"Nee." Micah was planning on catching up on letter writing and reading.

"We're hosting an ice-skating party on our lake out back. Everyone's invited. Esther is probably spreading the word as we speak, and we'd love to have you and your cousins come and share the day with us. We might even get a game of hockey together if we can push the kids off the ice long enough."

"Is the ice thick enough to support all the weight?"

"Oh ja. We went ice fishing the other day and had to drill down deep."

"Catch anything?"

"Nee, but it kept the boys out of Esther's hair for a couple of hours."

They laughed and talked about other things until the bell rang for them to get back to work. It was a long day, full of knocking down walls and hauling the debris out to the dumpster. Micah was hoping to talk to Lemuel on the ride home, but Lemuel was out like a light almost as soon as the van pulled onto the highway. He was still sleeping when Micah and his cousins got off at their stop.

Later, after they had washed up for supper, Aenti Judy handed him an envelope. "You got a letter from your Daed today."

"Thank you." He put it in his pocket to read later. He hoped it would be full of news about the family, but he doubted it. His mother's letters were usually full of that. His father was probably asking if Micah had met Betsy yet and reminding him that he needed to be home by April before they started the first planting. Daed was probably champing at the bit to get out and till the soil to prepare it for spring.

Amos led the nightly prayer and everyone passed around the hamburger casserole and roasted vegetables. Micah took a sweet potato roll as well.

"Betsy Miller made those," Judy said. "She gave them to me to share with you boys when I went to visit the bishop."

Micah smiled at his Aenti's not-so-subtle hint.

If she was expecting her sons to ask questions, she was going to be disappointed. They attacked the casserole as if they hadn't eaten in weeks. Micah couldn't blame them. It was delicious.

"How was work?" Aunt Judy asked.

"*Gut*," Amos managed in between bites.

Micah took pity on her. "We're making progress. The electricians are rewiring, so we were in a different part of the building than we have been."

"Was Lemuel Beachey there?"

"Ja, and Simon too. I didn't see much of them, but Simon invited all of us to go skating on the pond on Sunday."

Her face registered disbelief. "Lemuel is going to go skating?"

"I don't know about that, but the rest of us are." Micah signaled his cousins with his fork.

"You too, Amos?" His mother narrowed her eyes at him.

"Ja."

"*Gut.* I want you to spend some time with Candace."

Micah's jaw clenched involuntarily. He risked a glance at Amos, who appeared to be resigned instead of excited.

"Ja, Mamm," Amos droned.

"It's not like you are getting any younger."

The boys finished up their meals rather quickly after that and went off in various directions.

"And you," she said, when Micah reached for another roll. "Betsy Miller should be there as well. She's Candace's best friend. You should think about courting her."

"I haven't even been here a week, Aenti Judy. I'm still settling in. There's plenty of time between now and when I leave for home in the spring. Denki for a wonderful meal." He quickly left the table and returned to the room he was sharing with Amos before she could ask him anything else.

Micah set up his clothes for tomorrow and figured he had put off reading his father's letter long enough. Sitting down at the small writing table, he opened the letter. He smiled at his father's handwriting, and even though he didn't have high hopes about the letter, he felt a pang of homesickness at the sight.

Dear Micah,

I hope the weather has been mild for you up there. It's still cold here, and the long winter nights are starting to wear on me. I'm not built to sit and take it easy. I miss my gardens. Still, there are plenty of things to do around the farm. Your brothers and I recently fixed that hole in the roof of the barn, and not a moment too soon. The next day we got heavy snow.

Everyone is fine here. I'm hoping to plant beets as soon as the final frost is gone. I think it might be an early spring. Have you met anyone interesting? I'm told Betsy Miller is a good baker and keeps an organized house. Her father, Bishop Mark, is a fine man. I hope you are getting along with her.

I'm proud that you are making use of your time by pursuing work opportunities. It's that work ethic that will allow you to go far as a farmer. Your mother is eagerly awaiting a letter from you. Please get to that sooner rather than later.

Sincerely,

Ezekiel Zehr

Micah smiled that he didn't sign it *Daed*. He wrote so many letters that he probably used his own name out of habit. But then his smile faded. Would Daed be disappointed if Micah decided to step out with Candace instead? Or would that matter be overshadowed by Daed's wrath when Micah admitted he didn't want to be a farmer? Micah intended to use his land to build a woodworking shop and make cabinets.

He'd still have a garden. It just wouldn't be like the two-acre one that his father maintained. Or the full acre that his older brother planted and plowed. Or the five-acre plot that his other brother had, along with a dairy.

A light coming up the driveway caught his attention. They had visitors. It was a rather late hour for that, but the darkness made it seem later than it was. No one had retired to sleep yet, although Micah had been on his way.

He came downstairs to see who it was and broke out into a grin when he recognized Lemuel helping his daughter down from the buggy.

"Well I'll be," Judy murmured, opening the door. "Lemuel Beachey!" she called. "It's *gut* to see you. Come in." She nodded at Candace as they approached the porch. "Amos! Candace is here."

Micah hoped that Amos was in the barn, but he wasn't. Amos roused himself from the couch and joined them in the dining room.

"I wanted to bring over a cherry pie that I made," Candace said. "To thank Micah for helping us shovel when my father was ill."

"I'll go get some plates." Judy hustled into the kitchen.

"I'm so glad you came," Micah said, ostensibly to both their guests, but specifically to Candace. "How are the goats?" He tried not to be obvious about it, but he wanted to see her smile and hold her gaze again.

"They're great. They're much happier now that Daed and I shoveled their pen to give them more room to run around." She beamed up at her father.

Judy came back with dessert plates and forks.

"None for me," Lemuel said. "While we're here, I wanted to have a word with Micah."

Micah's heart sank. "Sure."

"Let's go outside." Lemuel turned abruptly and walked out.

With a helpless glance over his shoulder, he shrugged at Candace and went to get his coat. It was just his luck. Not only did he have to share a cherry pie with Amos, he had to abandon Candace to him while he talked to her father.

"Thank you for what you did the other day," Lemuel said without preamble. "The shoveling."

"It was my pleasure. I was sorry to hear you were under the weather."

Lemuel grunted. "I suppose. I spoke with the bishop yesterday."

He didn't think it was possible, but Micah's heart sank even lower. Lemuel was going to tell him that he heard that Micah was supposed to be courting Betsy and to stay away from Candace.

"The bishop wants me to take you on as an apprentice."

Micah's jaw dropped. The bishop must not have been talking with his father, then. "H-he did? That's surprising. I didn't think he knew I want to open my own shop."

"I don't know about that. But I guess it's time I went back to the shop. I could use your help getting it in order."

Micah was speechless. He would get to learn more of his craft—and see Candace every day. "I'd be honored."

Lemuel nodded. "Now, go back in and enjoy that pie before your cousins eat it all."

When they returned to the warmth of the kitchen, Judy and Candace were chatting. Amos had finished his pie and was clearly looking for an excuse to leave.

"Judy, may I speak with you in the parlor?" Lemuel asked.

Judy blinked in surprise, but smiled. "Sure."

Amos waited until his mother was out of sight and then excused himself. Micah slid into the chair across from Candace. "It's good to see you," he said.

"It's good to see you too."

They sat there just smiling at each other. Maybe it went on too long because she jumped up from her seat and abruptly grabbed a plate.

"Would you like some pie?" She cut him a slice.

"Ja. It looks great."

The pie was a perfect balance of tart and sweet. "This is wonderful. You didn't have to bring this, but I'm very glad you did. How is work?"

Candace shrugged. "It's been good. The snowstorm let me catch up on some chores at home. I'm off work tomorrow—and I'm looking forward to our pizza supper."

"Me too."

"Did Daed ask you about getting his workshop going again?"

"Ja. You'll be seeing a lot more of me."

"Well, you'll be having shepherd's pie on Saturday then."

"I look forward to it. And to talking with you more."

She bit her lip. "Micah, you know my best friend is Betsy, right?"

He nodded.

"And her father is the bishop?"

Micah nodded again, not sure where she was going with this.

"The rumor is that you've come to Randolph not just to work on this carpentry crew."

Now he understood. "Do you listen to gossip, Candace?"

"When you work where I do, it's hard to avoid it."

"My father does have plans for me. That's true. But I have my own plans, and so far, they don't seem to be aligned with his." He held her gaze steadily.

"Oh," she said, her cheeks flushing.

"I've also heard a rumor." Micah pushed his plate away and added sugar and milk to his tea.

"What's that?"

"That Amos's mother also has plans for him."

She gave a nervous giggle. "It's no rumor. She came right out and told me."

"How do you feel about it?"

"Ambivalent," she said honestly.

Ouch. Poor Amos. But Micah's prospects were looking up.

"I would hate to miss an opportunity because of gossip, wouldn't you?"

She smiled. "I'm not sure there are any opportunities here in Randolph."

"We'll see about that," he said. "But you're right. I've only been here a few days. There's no need to rush into decisions. I just wanted to let you know that there are no solid plans, and the only expectations seem to be our parents' and not our own."

Micah looked around to make sure none of his cousins were in hearing distance. "I would very much like the chance to get to know you better. How do you feel about that?" He held his breath while he waited for her answer, hoping she wouldn't say *ambivalent*—or something worse.

"I'd like that," she said and gave him a warm grin that felt like a ray of sunshine.

Amos came jogging back into the room and sat down quickly.

"What on earth?" Candace asked, staring at him.

At that moment, Lemuel and Judy came back in. Judy nodded at them approvingly. "It's good to see the young people having a nice talk. Too bad Betsy isn't here." Judy smiled at Micah.

Candace looked down at her hands.

"Denki for your hospitality, but we need to get home," Lemuel said. "Come along, Candace. We have things to do."

"Ja, Daed." She helped Judy carry the dishes to the sink. "Thanks again, Micah. I'll see you all on Sunday, right?"

"I wouldn't miss it," Micah said, walking them out. He made a bold move and helped Candace into the buggy. "I'll see you tomorrow." "Good night." She smiled shyly at him.

Micah watched until they turned the corner and he could no longer see the light coming from the buggy's lanterns.

He smiled as he remembered the touch of her hand. Tomorrow couldn't come soon enough for him.

7

Candace didn't want to get her hopes up, but Daed had gone to work two days in a row and was doing his morning chores. Maybe all he had needed was a visit from Bishop Mark to set him straight. She had the day off from work at the market, but unfortunately, she wasn't feeling so well today. After her father left for work, she had a whole list of things that she needed to do for the pizza supper tonight. She just couldn't do them. It was as if her boots were stuck to the floor and her head was stuffed with cotton.

The next thing she knew, she had gone back to bed and fallen into a deep sleep. It wasn't until Esther came in calling for her that she realized she had done so. Her bed was so warm and she was so tired. She considered not answering Esther, but she knew her sister-in-law would be worried.

"I'm upstairs cleaning." Candace felt guilty for the lie. But she was already ashamed that she had crawled back under the covers the moment she was alone. She didn't want to end up the way her father had been. But it was very easy to see why he'd done it. "I'll be right down." Candace tried to keep the reluctance out of her voice as she jammed her feet into her boots and hastily laced them up.

"Is everything all right?" Esther asked.

"Ja, I'm just tired that's all."

"How's the pizza dough coming?"

"What time is it?" Candace yawned as she came into the parlor.

"It's half past three. Gabriel should be home from school any time now."

Alarm and adrenaline shot through her. She didn't even remember having breakfast, and she'd slept right through lunch. Now there was no time to clean or even to make the pizza dough. She froze, then tears sprang into her eyes.

"I figured I'd stop by and see how things were going, and I'm glad I did. Sit." Esther steered her to the dining room table.

"I can't sit. I have too much to do."

Esther settled Abraham in the high chair Lemuel had made. He'd wanted his grandson to have one here and one at his own house. "Entertain the baby. You need to get some food into you and then we can come up with a plan."

"I don't know what's wrong with me," Candace whispered.

"I do. You've been pushing yourself, burning the candle at both ends since your Mamm died. Now that it's safe, it's all catching up to you."

"Safe?"

"You can relax a bit now that Lemuel is coming back to us."

"What if he relapses?"

"Then we'll handle it together. The way family does." Esther went into the kitchen. "I'm going to heat up the last of this soup and make you a sandwich. Then I'm going to make some oatmeal bars for a snack for Lemuel tomorrow. After you eat, we will make the dough for the pizza and then we're going to clean the house."

"I should be helping you," Candace said miserably. "Your Boppli—"

"You help me all the time. And now I'm helping you. It goes both ways, you know."

"Thank you." Candace rested her head on the table, but Abraham's happy chatter distracted her, and she raised her head to see what the baby was babbling about. He had a wooden train in his chubby fist and when he wasn't gnawing on it, he was running it all over the wooden tray. It gave her joy to watch him. She rummaged in Esther's baby bag and pulled out an arrowroot cookie.

"Here, chew on this. Not the train."

Abraham happily took it, and she went into the kitchen to wash the train.

"Is that bacon I smell?" she asked.

"I decided to make BLTs. I figured you were probably sick of bologna and eggs."

Her mouth watered at the thought. Too bad their home-grown tomatoes were long gone, but even with store tomatoes the sandwich would hit the spot. "That sounds perfect."

"Take this and go sit down. I'll be with you shortly."

Blowing on her soup, Candace took a cautious sip. It was rich and savory, and it warmed her from the inside out. Gradually, the fog lifted from her brain. By the time her sister-in-law brought their sandwiches, she was feeling like her old self.

Gabriel came barreling through the door, kicked off his boots and coat, and sat down at the table with them. "Can I have a sandwich?" he asked.

"That's why I made you one." Esther put one on a plate and set it in front of him. "Go get yourself a glass of milk. Then we're going to help Aenti Candace get the house ready for the pizza party."

With all three of them working—Gabriel mostly helped by entertaining the baby—the house was sparkling and the pizzas were lined up in the kitchen by the time the van dropped the men off that night after work.

Candace cast a critical eye over her father. He looked tired and stoic, but he seemed more himself. Simon hid a yawn while he greeted his family. Micah gave her a smile, and butterflies fluttered in her stomach.

"How was everything?" she asked.

"Busy. We worked hard," Micah said. He looked tired too. The long day and the long drive seemed to have sapped their energy.

"We'll be at it until spring. It's a good paycheck," her Daed said.

"Do you want supper right away?" Candace asked.

"Nee. We're stiff from sitting in the van. We'll take care of the animals and stretch our muscles a bit," Simon said. "If that's all right with you, Daed?"

Lemuel grunted.

"Well, you're going to need some fortifications." Esther brought out glasses of milk while Candace offered them the tray of oatmeal bars. After the quick snack, the men went outside to do the chores while Candace and Esther put the finishing touches on the apple pies for dessert.

"Denki for helping me today," Candace said to her sister-in-law. "Though I'm ashamed you had to. Come over tomorrow for lunch. I'm making ham and potato casserole."

"You don't have to do everything for everyone," Esther said, placing her hand on Candace's arm.

"What do you mean?"

"I mean, cheese pizza is fine and sandwiches would be fine for lunch tomorrow."

"I want to use up some potatoes. And I want to make a special meal for everyone."

"Everyone? Or is it because Micah will be here?" Esther teased.

Candace felt warmth creeping into her face. "Maybe both," she admitted.

Esther gave a small squeal and hugged her.

Once the men washed up from the chores, they all gathered around the table. They waited for Lemuel to start the prayer, but he didn't. After a long, awkward silence, Simon said the nightly supper prayer. Candace noticed that her father didn't say, "Amen" afterward with everyone else. That bothered her, but she didn't want to bring it up in front of Micah or the children.

Everybody dug into the pizzas, and she kept the cold drinks flowing while checking on her apple pies. It was a good thing she had shopped last night after work. Candace didn't know what had come over her today. She hoped it was like Esther had said and that her body and mind were just catching up after a long marathon of worry. She did wonder what her Mamm would have said about the pizza party. She hadn't been a fan of the dough and would pick off the cheese and toppings. Daed would help her by eating the crust.

The conversation was mostly about the weather predictions and the carpentry work. Esther and Candace excused themselves to do dishes. Candace set up the percolator for coffee.

"I wanted to thank you again. I couldn't have done this without you," she said.

"You would have found a way," Esther replied. "But I'm glad you didn't have to."

By the time they finished cleaning up, Gabriel had set up a board game on the dining room table and had roped his father and *Grossdaedi* into playing. Candace didn't have it in her for a long game and said as much when her nephew asked.

"I'll join you boys," Esther said. "Micah and Candace, why don't you do a crossword puzzle in the parlor where there's more room?"

Thank you, Esther.

Candace looked at Micah questioningly and he nodded. Feeling like a little girl on Christmas morning, she grabbed one of her Mamm's crossword books and sat on a pillow on the floor next to the low coffee table.

"You can sit on the couch, but I find it's easier to reach from a pillow on the floor."

"Sounds good."

She tossed him one. Flicking through the completed puzzles, she felt a twinge of nostalgia at seeing her mother's handwriting. She found a fresh puzzle and pulled out a pencil from the table's drawer. "I'm happy that you're here. It's nice to have some fun in this house again."

"What was your Mamm like?"

The pencil fell from her fingers, and she gaped at him. No one ever asked about her Mamm.

"If you'd rather not talk about her, I understand," Micah said kindly.

"Nee, it's not that. It's just that I haven't talked about her in so long, even though she's always in my thoughts and still very much a presence in my life. I don't know where to begin. It's hard because you never knew her."

"I know her name was Sarah. And I know her secret ingredient for brownies."

"How?" Candace asked, surprised. She picked up the pencil again.

"Your Daed told me her name, and Gabriel spilled the beans about the instant coffee."

"Daed talked about her to you?" She couldn't believe it. Her father wasn't a chatty man, and he could barely say her mother's name. If he was opening up to Micah about her, Micah was truly a gift from Gött.

"Just a little bit. What's the first clue?" He indicated the puzzle.

"Four letter word. Jacob's brother."

"Esau," Micah supplied.

She wrote it down. There were a few more easy words that she filled in. It also gave her a little more time to think about how she was going to answer Micah's question.

Finally, one of the clues stumped her, and she handed Micah the puzzle. "Mamm loved to sing," she said quietly. "Everything from Christmas carols to prayer hymns, and even some Englisch songs we heard from our neighbors in the summer. I swear, their radio stations play the same five songs over and over again. You try not to listen, but they get into your head."

"Ja, the Englisch call them 'earworms.' We get them too. I went to a concert when I was on *Rumspringa*. I saw the Armchair Professors in Lancaster."

"I don't know them."

"You've probably heard their songs. They're on the radio all the time."

"Sing one for me."

He reddened. "I couldn't carry a tune if it had a handle." He filled in some more blocks before handing the puzzle back to her.

"Mamm liked to bake," Candace continued. "She was always going to the library and taking out magazines and cookbooks to find new recipes that she could play around with. I've got a whole box filled with her notes and sketches." She squinted at a clue that was bothering her. She should know this one. "What's a five-letter word for love?"

"Agape."

She blushed and added it in.

"Have you ever thought of maybe typing them up and publishing a booklet? I think others might like to benefit from your Mamm's knowledge."

She gaped at him in amazement. "Nee, it never occurred to me."

"A few of the ladies back home have done that. They bring it to an Englisch printer and he makes spiral-bound copies. They sell theirs, but you could just keep it around for family."

"That sounds like a really nice remembrance to have of her," Candace said, thoughtfully. "She would have gotten a real kick out of it too. I bet my boss, Karen, at the Amish Market would let me sell it with my soaps and lotions."

"Does the market sell them on consignment or buy them outright?"

"On consignment. I have special numbers on them, and at the end of the month, the office runs a report and pays me for the amount sold. The market takes a cut, of course. I usually have a pretty good idea how much it will be, but they need the computers to tell them."

"Do you sell a lot of them?"

"It depends on what you mean by a lot. I sell enough that I have some pin money, but not enough that it could be my full-time job." She wanted to tell him about the goat yoga, but she didn't want him to laugh at her. "I really like your idea about the recipe book. I think Betsy has an old typewriter I could borrow. Her Daed writes a column about Randolph for *The Budget* on it."

He smiled. "I'd like to help, but I'm no good at typing."

"Don't worry. You've helped plenty."

They went back and forth for a while, filling in the boxes of the crossword. She could hear Gabriel and Abraham giggling in the next room and the rumble of her father's voice. The wood crackling on the fire gave a peaceful warmth to the room, and Candace felt something in her ease and relax.

Esther brought them two slices of pie. When Candace started to make a move to jump up and take over, Esther laid a hand on her shoulder. "You stay here. It's all set. Would you like coffee, tea, or milk?"

"Milk, please," Micah said.

"Me too. I shouldn't have coffee this late."

When Esther brought over the glasses, she said, "We're going to head on home. Is there anything else you need me to do?"

Candace shook her head. "You've done so much already."

"I'll see you tomorrow." Esther smiled at Micah. "Have a nice night."

After they left, Lemuel came into the living room and eased into his chair. "Do you want to help us with the puzzle, Daed?" she asked.

"Nee, I'm going to read for a bit." He lit the propane lamp by his chair and settled in with the paper.

Candace was afraid to start talking about her Mamm again. She didn't know why, but she felt that it might cause him to relapse. Micah figured out the last few words on his own. She probably could have helped, but she was distracted and a little uneasy with her father in the room. She had become so used to being alone, and before that, there was always her Mamm singing or chattering. She didn't know how to make it feel normal with just the two of them. Her Daed's silent presence in the corner set her on edge. Maybe it would get better with time.

"It's getting late," Micah said. "I should get going."

"I'll go hitch up the buggy," Candace said, getting up.

"That's all right. I can walk. It's not that far. I'll take that shortcut through the cow paths by the bishop's house that you took the other day. Simon showed me how you did it."

"Nonsense," she said. "It's pitch-dark and cold out. It'll only take me a minute."

"All right," he said.

Candace waited for her father to offer to drive Micah, but he seemed lost in his newspaper. But since he hadn't turned the page in fifteen minutes, she was sure his mind was elsewhere.

However, once they were riding into the darkness, Candace was glad that she had a little more time to spend with Micah.

"We seemed to have talked about my family all night. I don't know anything about yours," Candace said.

"I've got three younger sisters and three brothers, two older and one younger. The older ones are farmers like my Daed and the younger one is building a dairy farm. My Daed is hoping I become a farmer too, but it doesn't interest me. He hasn't accepted that yet."

"Is that why you took the carpentry job up here?" she asked.

"Ja. I figured it would give him time to get used to the idea. I'm surprised that Bishop Mark is supporting me wanting to learn more of the woodworking craft."

"You can't farm in the winter. That's what Daed always said. It's a seasonal job." She wished it was a nice spring night when nine thirty at night would be dark, but not winter-dark, as if it was midnight.

"Have you ever had to do anything against your parents' wishes?" he asked.

Candace thought about it. "I'm sure I must have, but nothing that comes to mind. My mother loved our goats, so she encouraged me to make my soaps and lotions from their milk. I wanted to take it a step further and maybe make a petting zoo or another type of entertainment." She still couldn't tell him about the goat yoga. She was afraid of appearing silly to him. "I think she would have preferred that I sold my things out of our home, but we don't have the tourists that Pennsylvania does. Are your farms close to the main tourist areas?"

"Nee, but there are plenty of bus tours that come by. My father has a parking lot for them, and he takes them on a tour of the farm."

"I should send you home with a box of soap and hand cream so he can show them that too," she said.

"Maybe you and your family could come visit in the spring?" he suggested. She glanced at him in surprise, but he kept his eyes on the road. "Gabriel and Abraham would love playing with my brothers' Kinner."

"That might be a nice trip for my Daed," she said, even though her heart was thumping wildly. "Esther and Simon would probably want to stay home with the new baby, but we could bring Gabriel and Abraham. It would be a *gut* experience for them."

She took the roads instead of the back pastures because, even though it was cold in the buggy, she wasn't in a hurry.

"I could show your Daed around my workshop, but it's not as large and well stocked as his," he said.

"Yet."

"The problem is that my Daed still thinks it's a hobby."

"He'll come around. After all, it's not as if your family has a shortage of farmers."

Micah chuckled. "That's true."

All too soon, she was driving up the Eichers' driveway. She spotted Amos climbing the porch and felt oddly guilty. When he recognized her, guilt flashed over his face too. Candace didn't know why either of them were uncomfortable.

"Think about what I said, about coming to visit in the spring," Micah said as he climbed down from the buggy.

Candace wasn't sure she would be able to think about anything else. She wasn't quite ready to step out with Micah, even if he did ask her instead of Betsy. With her father so volatile and Esther about to give birth, she couldn't think about courtship right now. But soon. If he asked her in the spring, she would gladly step out with him. Until then, she was thankful for little moments like this where she could see him smile.

But what if Betsy wanted to marry Micah? She would never hurt her best friend by stealing someone she was interested in. Shifting those thoughts away, Candace decided that she would worry about that if and when she had to.

8

Micah helped his cousins with their regular chores then shoveled more snow. The snowbanks were piling up so high he didn't think they were going to melt until May. Then he asked Amos for a ride to the Beachey farm. Judy was more than happy to let Amos take him and pick him up.

"Make sure you talk with Candace, Amos," she said.

"Ja, Mamm," Amos said unenthusiastically.

"And if you take the cow pasture roads, you can stop by the bishop's house and visit with Betsy for a bit, Micah."

"She's probably at work," Micah hedged.

"Nee," Amos chimed in. "She goes in late on Saturdays."

"There you have it." Judy waved them off.

"How do you know Betsy's hours so well?" Micah asked once they were out of earshot.

Amos shrugged. "Just do."

"I'd like to ask you something."

Amos shrugged again.

"I know I've only been here a week and it's probably too soon to make any decisions about the future, but . . ."

"I know what you're going to say."

"I don't think you do," Micah said.

"Mamm already told me that you and Betsy were going to step out in the spring."

Micah tried not to grit his teeth. "I barely know Betsy."

"She's a great girl," Amos said, perking up. "She makes the best fry pies you'll ever taste. My favorite is the coconut cream."

Micah had to admit that did sound good.

"She's also got a green thumb. She can plant anything and make it grow. She once grew a pineapple."

"Really?" Micah squinted at him in disbelief.

"It took three years. But she babied those seedlings under a dome, keeping them in the kitchen by the stove or up in her room when it was cold. After all that work, the pineapple was only the size of a child's fist, but it wasn't sour at all."

"It sounds like you know her pretty well."

"She's my best friend." Amos stared stoically ahead of him.

"Why haven't you ever asked her to step out?"

"Her father told me not to bother. And he's the bishop."

Micah frowned. "Why would he do that?"

"He said that Betsy's dream was to live near Lancaster by her sister Susan and to open a bakery with her."

"What did Betsy say?"

"I know she doesn't like working at the Amish Market."

"Why not?"

"It's too fast-paced. She'd rather stay home, but there's not much money coming in during the winter, so she has to work. I think she'd be great owning her own bakery. I don't see why it needs to be near Susan, though. I had hoped that when Betsy didn't go visit her sister this summer she might have changed her mind about Pennsylvania."

"And then I showed up," Micah said.

"And then you showed up," Amos repeated.

"What do you think about Candace?"

"She's nice. She plays a mean game of volleyball. You do not want to be across the net from her. She can bake too. That cherry pie of hers was the best I've ever tasted. Don't tell Betsy I said that."

"I won't. What if I told you that I was thinking of asking Candace to step out instead of Betsy?"

Amos looked thoughtful. "I think you'd make a few people a little annoyed with you."

Amos had the gift of understatement.

"Would you be one of them?" Micah asked.

"I wouldn't want to see Betsy get hurt."

"If another suitor asked her to step out before I even had a chance to, then I don't see how she would."

"Like who? All your brothers are already married."

Micah poked him in the arm. "You. Why not you?"

"Her Daed said not to bother."

"Maybe you should let Betsy tell you not to bother."

"But my Mamm wants me to step out with Candace."

"Why?"

"She thinks she can save Lemuel from himself if we're part of the family. She says she knows what he's going through and he needs some help to get right again."

"I think Lemuel can save himself, but if all she wants is an excuse to visit him, we can both take her over there."

Amos considered his words.

They passed by the Miller farm, and Betsy came out on the porch. She beamed and waved at them. Amos stopped the buggy.

"How are you today?" she asked.

Micah tipped his hat at her and Amos said, "I'm taking Micah to see Candace."

"Her father, actually," Bishop Mark said, coming out onto the porch to stand next to his daughter.

"Ja," Micah said. "We're going to clean out his workshop and maybe get started on some projects."

"Would you like a ride over to visit with Candace?" Amos asked.

Betsy opened her mouth to answer, but her father answered for her. "We need her here this afternoon. We have some chores to catch up on."

"Besides," Betsy said, "I've got some baking to do for our ice-skating party tomorrow."

Amos's face brightened.

"I heard you make the best coconut cream fry pies in all of New York," Micah said.

Betsy grinned. "Well, I don't know about that."

"We'll have to bring some over tomorrow." Bishop Mark beamed in approval.

"I'm looking forward to it." Micah waved as Amos got the horse moving again.

"He seemed awfully glad to see you," Amos muttered.

"Tomorrow, ask Betsy if she's really looking to move to Pennsylvania to open a bakery with her sister or if she wouldn't mind doing that in Randolph."

"What are you going to do?"

"I'm going to see if Candace will help me get her Daed and Aenti Judy together to talk and visit more often."

"You sound like my Mamm, playing matchmaker."

"If they're too busy with other, then they won't have time for you and me, will they?"

"But the bishop—"

"One step at a time, Amos." Not to mention Micah had his own father thrown into the mix of people to smooth things over with as well. While he was sure his father wouldn't care which girl Micah wound up marrying, he would care that the acres he intended to give Micah wouldn't be used as farmland. His father wanted him to grow tobacco, but planting, harvesting, drying leaves, and maintaining plants simply didn't appeal to him. He didn't mind helping out at his brothers' farms. If it was going to be his daily work, though, Micah wanted something that he enjoyed doing. And just like he planned on asking the woman of *his* choice to marry him, Micah planned on spending his life fulfilling his dream. He shouldn't have to worry about disobeying his parents or disappointing them with his decisions.

Amos dropped Micah off in front of the Beachey farm, waving at Candace when she came out on the porch. "Will you be done around three?" Amos asked.

"Better make it four." Micah jumped down from the buggy. "Are you sure you don't want to stay and help out?"

Candace leaned on the porch railing. "You're welcome to stay. I've just baked some rolls."

"I would," Amos said, "but I promised Mamm I'd help my brothers give the barn a good cleaning."

"Should I help too?" Micah asked.

Amos shook his head. "You're on a mission from the bishop to help Lemuel. You're exempt."

"Lucky me."

Amos snorted and with another wave to Candace, he turned the buggy around and headed back home.

"Guder Mariye," Candace said. "Have you eaten breakfast?"

"I did. It's good to see you. I enjoyed doing the puzzle with you last night." He smiled at her as she welcomed him into the house.

"I'm looking forward to doing another one with you," she said. "You're much more helpful with them than Gabriel."

He laughed. "I hope so. Is your father well?"

"Ja, he's out in the workshop if you want to join him."

Micah would rather spend his day with Candace, but he figured she had chores to do, and he was there for another reason. "I'll see you soon."

Walking out toward the workshop, he noticed little goats chasing each other around the pasture and bleating with joy. It was a mild January day, but still cold enough that they didn't lounge on the ground for very long. They were adorable. No wonder Candace loved them.

Peeking into the warehouse, he saw Lemuel wiping down the countertops. "Hello," he said. "Grab a rag and let's clean up some of the dust and grime."

They worked in silence for several minutes before Lemuel spoke to him again. "What type of cabinets were you looking to make?"

"When I was on Rumspringa, I worked with an Englisch furniture maker. He mainly glued his pieces together."

Lemuel made a noise of disgust.

"Exactly. But I used some power tools and got some experiences I wouldn't have gotten otherwise. I figure I'm ready to start learning more of the craft. Maybe we could start with a chair. I was admiring the ones you made in the kitchen."

"Those should be easy enough as a first project. But first, I want you to practice joints. Some glue is necessary, but I'm willing to bet your Englisch boss was using too much. I'm going to teach you mortise-and-tenon, dovetail, and tongue-and-groove."

"I've some experience with the last two," Micah said.

"The bishop wants me to teach you how to make a kitchen table and chairs for his daughter."

"Betsy?"

"Ja. As part of her dowry. I was thinking of Mission style over Shaker, but I imagine that's your choice, as is the wood we use."

"My choice?" Micah bit back a groan. Now, it made sense. The bishop thought he was getting his future son-in-law to make his own kitchen set. "I think there's been a misunderstanding or at least a miscommunication. I'll be happy to make Betsy furniture for her wedding, but I don't have a say in the style or color."

"Is that so? Smart man. Wives care about these things more than we do."

For a moment, Micah thought things were good, but then Lemuel seemed to realize what he'd said and looked stricken.

"Did you make your own kitchen set?"

"Of course I did," he said gruffly and turned away.

"What style did Sarah want?"

Lemuel flinched at his wife's name. He closed his eyes and forced out the answer. "She wanted Mission style in oak with a tobacco-brown stain."

"Sounds good to me." Perhaps someday Candace would like kitchen furniture similar to what she'd grown up with. He stopped himself. This furniture was for Betsy. Well, hopefully she'd like this kind too. "Once we're done with that," he continued, "can we work on some kitchen cabinets?"

Lemuel nodded.

But before they could do anything else, they needed to finish cleaning the shop. It clearly hadn't been used in months, and there was a thin layer of dust covering everything. Lemuel didn't say another word until they had scrubbed and polished every inch of the space. Once that was done, Lemuel had him clean the tools while he took inventory of the wood he had.

"We might have to take a ride into the lumberyard next payday," Lemuel said.

"All right." That sounded good to him.

They worked to get things in order until Gabriel came in to tell them that lunch was ready.

They washed up and joined Simon and his family and Candace at the table. The smell of fresh bread and melting butter was strong in the dining room and Micah's stomach growled. As they sat down, Micah centered himself for prayer.

After a long pause, Candace said, "Daed, would you lead us in prayer?"

"Nee."

Micah opened up his eyes in shock. Candace's eyes filled with tears, but Simon jumped in and said grace. He noticed that Lemuel didn't say amen after the prayer and his heart sank. It looked like Aenti Judy might be right about Lemuel having a crisis of faith.

Candace wouldn't look at her father as she passed the dish of shepherd's pie around the table, followed by thick, buttery slices of toasted bread. Even the salad was special, with a poppy seed dressing and pumpernickel croutons. But there was a part of him that was uneasy in the stilted conversation.

Lemuel ate his meal and drank his iced tea as if nothing out of the ordinary was going on. After lunch, he excused himself and went back out to the workshop without a word to anyone. Simon followed his father.

"I think we're going to head back home for our afternoon naps," Esther said with a tired smile. "Unless you need us?"

"No, that's all right. I've got this. I'm going to work on my soaps this afternoon."

"Great," Esther said. "Micah, it was lovely to see you again."

"And you as well."

Candace gathered up the empty plates and took them back to the kitchen. Micah didn't want to intrude on a family conversation if that was why Simon had gone out to the workshop with Lemuel, so he helped Candace clear the table.

"Can I help?" he asked. "How about I dry?" He grabbed a towel and waited by the sink.

"Shouldn't you be out in the workshop with Daed?"

"I have a feeling Simon and he are talking about private matters."

She bit her lip. "I hope so. I'm sorry you had to see that. I'm a little worried about what it means."

"Simon will get to the bottom of it. If need be, maybe one of the deacons can talk to your Daed. Or maybe the bishop."

Candace scrubbed a plate before rinsing it off and handing it to him to dry. "I just want things to go back to normal." She sounded frustrated. "But I don't even know what normal is at the moment."

"It's okay. Grief can take on many forms, and it's different for everyone." He dried the plate and set it on the counter, not knowing where it was supposed to go.

"Have you lost someone close to you?" she asked.

He sighed. "Ja, my littlest sister. Her name was Sarah too. She got sick. We thought it was just a cold. But it was worse. She started having trouble breathing and—" He swallowed hard. "It was pneumonia. She went quickly. Too quickly. She was only six."

The plate she was washing slipped through her soapy fingers, but he caught it before it crashed into the counter or the sink. "I'm so sorry," she whispered. "Your poor parents."

"They had a rough time. So I understand Lemuel's grief."

"Did they ever renounce their faith?"

"Not in my hearing, but I suppose there might have been a time when the world seemed so dark that it could have happened."

Candace took the plate from him and continued washing it. "How did your family recover?"

"Slowly."

She gave a watery sniffle. "More than three months?"

"It's been three years and it's still hard. There are days when I automatically look for her to come skipping home from school. I'd like to tell you that the grief goes away, but it never really does. It just becomes a part of you, and you learn to live with it. Some days it doesn't hurt at all to remember her. It was the guilt that got to me. I should have been closer. One of us should have been watching her better. As if simply being there would have stopped it."

"Well, that's one thing that my Daed was spared. He was right next to her in the garden." She pointed out back. "They were picking the last of the corn. She said something about the heat and the next minute she was gone." Candace handed him the plate and wiped her face on the towel next to her.

"It's *gut* to get the tears out. I think Lemuel's anger with Gött is really sadness."

"What can I do for him?" she asked, continuing with the dishes.

"Just keep doing what you have been. Be there to support him, but take care of yourself first. You and Simon are doing a good job of supporting each other."

She blew out a shaky breath. "I'm terrified of what's going to happen after Esther has the baby. They're going to be so busy. I'm going to have to be on top of everything, and it's going to be tough working full-time and taking care of Daed. If he can work even with his grief, I think we'll all get through it. But I'll be honest, it keeps me up at night thinking about it."

"If you need me, come get me or send word. For anything." He meant it. He would be there for her in a heartbeat.

"I appreciate that, Micah. I know we haven't known each other long, but you've been such a good friend." She finished up the dishes and then put away what he'd dried. "I went through some of Mamm's recipes last night before bed. There are a lot of them. But it was good to see her handwriting and remember the good times."

"Maybe that's what your father needs. To remember the good times so his grief doesn't overshadow them."

"I'm not sure how to help him with that."

"I don't know either, but I think we can help him together. I know that all of Randolph wants him to get better."

Candace nodded. "That helps so much. Do you think I should try to take him to see a doctor?"

"It couldn't hurt. But if he's anything like my Daed, he's not going to want to spend the money or take the time off from work."

"I think that would be his response too."

"The worst he can do is say no."

Simon slammed the door when he came back in the house and Candace jumped in reaction. "We have a problem," he said. "Micah, I'm sorry to involve you in this."

"It's all right," he said. "Candace and I were just discussing your father. Do you want me to go out and see if he'll talk with me?"

"Nee, he needs some time to calm down. We had strong words." Simon took off his hat and ran his fingers through his hair. "He says he's not going to church anymore."

"He has to," Candace said. "Bishop Mark will get angry, if he isn't already."

"I'm going to talk to the bishop now and see if he can come over and talk some sense into him."

"Nee," Candace said, grabbing Simon's arm. "The Millers are coming over to your house for the skating party tomorrow anyway. Let's wait until then and see if a good night's sleep will change his mind. Getting the bishop involved now will only upset him more, and you know he digs in his heels when he's already angry."

Simon shook his head. "Time won't help. You didn't hear him."

"Let's just wait until after tomorrow. Please, Simon."

Micah shifted uncomfortably. "I can see if my Aenti Judy will talk with him as well. If might be helpful for him to hear from someone who's lost a spouse."

"All right," Simon said reluctantly. "But I want it settled before we have church again."

"We all do," Candace soothed.

Simon turned to Micah. "I should take you home. When my Daed gets into a mood, he's not fit company. At least he's in his workshop instead of his bedroom. That's something."

"Ja, it is."

"Can you stay for dessert?" Candace asked. "Both of you?"

"Save it for tomorrow. We'll be feeding a lot of hungry mouths," Simon said.

"True." Candace turned to Micah. "Hopefully we can put all this bad stuff behind us and concentrate on having a little fun tomorrow. I'll see you then."

"Thank you for a delicious lunch. It was a real treat. You're a good cook."

"Denki." She flushed prettily.

Micah would make sure they had plenty of time to talk about nice things tomorrow. He followed her brother into his yard and helped him with the horse and buggy. Simon took the back roads and when they passed the bishop's farm, Micah caught a glimpse of Betsy and Amos talking by the barn. But Amos's horse and buggy were nowhere in sight. He must have walked back just to talk with her.

Micah was glad he didn't have to sneak around to see Candace. But he would have to face his own father sooner rather than later about becoming a farmer. And he wasn't looking forward to that confrontation. Compared to that, helping Lemuel Beachey in his grief seemed a much easier task.

9

When Candace woke up, she felt like a black cloud of dread was hovering over her head. Would her father retreat to his bedroom or would he continue to take small steps to overcome his grief? She knocked on his door before she went downstairs and got no answer. Closing her eyes, she rested her forehead on the door. She couldn't live like this.

"Daed, I'm coming in." She opened the door.

The room was empty, and the bed was made. She walked slowly into the room. It was cold. The woodstove was cold to the touch. The fire hadn't been lit last night, and her Daed hadn't made the bed. He hadn't slept in it at all.

Panic flared through her. She flew down the stairs calling for him. What if he'd had a coronary last night and was lying somewhere on the ground, like Mamm? What if he'd died with his back to Gött?

When she burst out the back door in her stocking feet, she saw him mucking out the barn.

Holding her hand over her stomach, she fought nausea. The cold air slapping her face in the predawn morning helped clear her thoughts until only the slow burn of anger remained. Jamming her feet into her boots, she grabbed her jacket and stormed over to him.

"Where did you sleep last night?" Candace demanded.

"I fell asleep on the couch."

She paused in her outrage. "I was worried when you weren't in your room."

"Is breakfast ready yet?" he asked.

Thrown by his casual tone, she paused to center herself. "Not quite yet. Eggs and bacon sound good? You're going to need the extra fuel for skating."

"There's a lot of work that needs to be done around here."

"Please, Daed. Your grandsons are looking forward to you skating with them."

He sighed and shoveled more hay. "All right."

Happy at that little victory, even if it was a bit manipulative, Candace went to the hen house to see how generous the ladies were feeling today. She was pleased to leave with an apron full of eggs.

By the time she finished frying the eggs and bacon, Daed had finished his chores and was seated at the table. She poured them both a cup of coffee and served breakfast. He dug in right away.

"Daed," she said softly, "don't you want to lead the morning prayer?"

"Don't you start too. I heard enough from your brother last night."

"Can you at least tell me why you have stopped praying?"

He shook his head. "Why bother when no one is listening?"

Tears flooded her eyes. "He's listening, Daed. He listens to me every day."

"Well, He's stopped listening to me. I haven't felt Him since your mother died."

She placed her hand on his. "What did the bishop say when you told him that?"

"I didn't mention it to him."

"I think he could help."

"Is he going to bring your mother back?"

"Daed," she said, scandalized.

"Then he's not going to help. I'm not hungry." He scraped back his chair and went back outside.

Candace didn't know what to do. Her whole life revolved around service and loving Gött. Their community was strong in their faith and came together in times of joy and grief. Today was supposed to be joyous. Maybe he would see that and come back toward the light. She would pray to that end.

No longer hungry herself, she cleaned away the plates and saved the eggs and bacon for sandwiches later. She busied herself making a large picnic lunch for all of them. Then she dug out both her and her Daed's skates and made sure the blades were still good. After making several thermoses of coffee and hot cocoa, she trudged over to her brother's house to see if she could help with the preparations. Last night she had baked some of her mother's tried-and-true recipes to feel closer to her. She was pleased with how they came out and was definitely going to include them in her recipe booklet, which she was beginning to suspect would turn into a full book.

Simon was out by the pond making sure everything was safe, and Gabriel was already practicing his hockey moves. She set her basket and the coffee on the picnic table and set their skates on the ground next to it. Going inside, she found Esther putting the finishing touches on some cookie trays.

"Are you sure we have enough food?" Candace asked.

"Everyone's bringing a picnic lunch, so it's just the desserts. I always like to have extra for the Kinner."

"Are you sure you're up to this?"

"I'm not going skating, if that's what you mean." Esther rubbed her stomach. "I'm going to be in a camping chair with my blankets and knitting, which will just happen to be next to these chocolate chip cookies." She snuck one out from under the plastic wrap. "They're still warm. Want one?"

A cookie sounded like a great idea and she helped herself. It was gooey and chocolatey, and it shouldn't have made her feel better, but it did. "When's everyone coming over?"

"In about an hour. I'm glad the snow held off so we can do this. I think everyone needed a little break from the weather and the inside of our own houses. I know I've missed seeing everyone out and about."

Candace had to agree. Maybe all her father needed was some fresh air, some chocolate chip cookies, and some fun times with their community. She knew he wouldn't magically go back to normal after one day, but she could hope it would help.

She and Esther tidied the kitchen and then carried the cookies and more hot chocolate out to the picnic tables. By the time they had gotten everything done, people were beginning to trickle in.

There was no sign of her father, and Simon was missing too. She hoped he had gone to the house to smooth things over after their argument last night. Candace soon forgot about her father and brother as a rush of Kinner ran out to the ice and started dividing up into hockey teams. The younger children and their parents stayed by Candace and the cookies. They were content to play in the snow and then warm up with hot chocolate.

Candace got her skates on and headed for a section of the pond that didn't have racing boys with hockey sticks. She practiced her figure eights and did a few laps. After many months of just work, chores, and sleep, it was freeing to glide across the ice.

A few moments later, Betsy skated out to join her and promptly fell. "I forgot how awful I am at this," she said ruefully.

"You just have to get used to it and stop bending your ankles. You're going to break them."

"If I could put the blades on my ankles I'd do just fine."

Candace braced herself and helped Betsy to her feet. She held her hands and skated backward while Betsy tried to stay upright. "Come on. I taught Gabriel how to skate like this. You can do it too."

"Gabriel is a lot closer to the ground than I am. Whoa!" This time when she fell, she took Candace down as well. "Ouch. I banged my elbow," Betsy said, rubbing it. "Is it cocoa time yet?"

"The ice is hard." Candace wasn't sure she would be able to get up gracefully.

"Well, that's why we're skating and not swimming."

"You're grumpy today."

"I think I'm going to crawl to the edge and go build a snowman with the Kinner."

"Don't look now, but I think we've got reinforcements coming." Candace waved at Amos and Micah, who were gliding toward them as if they'd been born to skate.

"Everyone okay?" Amos asked.

Micah reached down and helped her up, steadying her when she almost overbalanced. Amos had his hands full with Betsy.

"Watch it, Amos," Candace said, giggling. "She's a menace on the ice."

"I'd better hold your hand to make sure you keep your balance," Amos said to Betsy.

Candace noticed that Micah's gloved hand still held her elbow. She glanced back at the house, but no one seemed to be paying any attention to them as more families arrived. "Let's skate out farther," she suggested.

"How far?" Betsy asked. "Because we have to skate back, you know."

Could they skate all the way to Pennsylvania? Or maybe to Florida. "Just far enough that we don't get hit with the hockey puck and to make some room for the other skaters." They skated farther down the pond, going almost to the opposite end.

"Simon checked that it's all solid, right?" Micah asked, his brow furrowing.

"Ja," she said. "There's nothing to worry about."

"Where is Simon? I didn't see him."

"I think he's with Daed."

"How did that go last night after I left?"

"Not well. Let's not talk about it."

"Whatever you wish," Micah grabbed her hand and took off down the ice. She kept up with him, then stopped and whirled him around. He laughed and did it back. They spun around in circles until they were both dizzy and laughing. Candace had to lean on him for support as her equilibrium centered again.

Amos and Betsy were off on their own. They were still in sight, but out of earshot.

"Was it something I said?" Candace said with a grin.

"I think Betsy was afraid Amos was going to try that with her." Amos and Betsy were staggering around the ice. He was trying valiantly to keep her from falling again.

Candace felt a pang of guilt. Micah was supposed to be there for Betsy and she was spending time with him. That wasn't right. "We should probably skate back in. I should check on Esther, especially if Simon is with my Daed."

"Should we help those two?" Micah asked. Amos was slowly guiding Betsy back as well.

"Nee, I'm afraid we'll upset the balance and we'll all wind up face-first on the ice."

As they skated slowly back, curiosity got the better of her. "Do you know why the bishop and your Daed are matchmaking you and Betsy?"

"I'll have to ask my Daed, but something Amos said might be the key to it. He said that Betsy wanted to move close to Lancaster to start a bakery with her sister."

"With Susan?" Candace grimaced. "Betsy would rather move to Antarctica and wrestle polar bears than go into business with her sister."

"That's awfully specific. Have you discussed this with Betsy?"

"In a way. Susan is . . ." Candace had to remind herself to be kind. "Well, she has been known to bully her younger sister and is very controlling. To be honest, we were all glad when she fell in love during her Rumspringa and moved to your neck of the woods."

"Why would her father think that she wanted to go work with her sister?"

"Susan was their favorite. They didn't see her prickly nature the way we did. I imagine she put the idea in her parents' head. She's probably a little lonely without her family around her. I know I'd be lost without Simon and Esther."

"Oh," Micah said softly.

As they neared the Kinner playing hockey, Candace eased away from Micah and made sure they weren't holding hands. She didn't want to upset Bishop Mark since he harbored thoughts of Betsy and Micah together.

"That was fun," she said. "Care for some hot cocoa?"

"I think that will hit the spot."

She poured him a cup and took one for herself. She noticed Esther looking cold and miserable.

"Why don't you go inside and warm up? Take it easy by the fire."

"I can't. Not with all these people here."

"Go," Candace urged. "I'll watch the boys."

"Are you sure?"

"We'll be fine."

"If you see Simon, have him come and see me." Esther said, hauling herself to her feet.

The camp chair was so low, Micah and Candace had to help her out of it. "I've got some beef stew simmering for supper," Candace said. "I'll bring some over so you don't have to worry about cooking."

"Bless you. I'm just so tired lately."

Candace watched as Esther made her way into the house.

"Do you want me to see if I can find Simon or your Daed?" Micah asked.

It was a tough choice. She would have loved to have them here enjoying the winter picnic that Simon was supposed to be hosting, but it was also nice not to have to worry about what other people would think or do if Daed decided to say those horrifying things about the church. She could only hope he was repenting his angry words and that Simon was there for him.

"Nee, they'll be around. Try some of the cookies before the Kinner eat them all. The chocolate caramel rounds are one of my Mamm's recipes."

The rest of the afternoon went by in a whirl of snowball fights and a contest of the best snowman, judged by the bishop. He gave out peppermint sticks to everyone who entered, and the winner got an orange and a chocolate bar.

By the time everyone began rounding up their Kinner and heading for home to prepare for another work week, there was still no sign of her brother and father. When Candace brought Abraham in for his nap, she found Esther fast asleep on the couch.

Gabriel was still on the ice. He would sleep well tonight. Micah had stuck close, but not close enough to capture unwanted attention. Luckily, Betsy and Amos sat with them, and they all chatted together in between activities.

She was down by the pond helping Gabriel take off his skates when Simon showed up. But before she could call out to him, he made a beeline for the bishop. After a short but intense conversation, the bishop followed Simon back to the barn.

"What's going on?" Gabriel asked.

"I'm not sure."

"I haven't seen Daed or Grossdaedi all day. Do you think they're building something in the woodshop?"

"Maybe."

"Should I go see?" Micah murmured.

She nodded, afraid her father had retreated back to his bedroom. As everyone said their final goodbyes, Candace started cleaning up. Betsy and her mother joined in.

Candace invited Betsy and her Mamm into Simon's house and made a pot of tea. While it was coming to a boil, she resisted the urge to run back home to see what was going on. Esther joined them in the dining room.

"I'm so sorry I slept the day away." Esther rubbed her eyes.

"I was the same way before I had Betsy," Rachel Miller said.

Candace saw that she had left her thermoses outside, so she excused herself and went out to bring them in before she forgot them. If she didn't, they'd likely have snow tonight and she wouldn't find them again until spring.

As she was about to go back inside, she saw the bishop coming back alone. She walked up to him. "Is everything all right?"

Bishop Mark shook his head grimly. "It's worse than I thought. He's an obstinate man and I'm running out of choices."

Fear flashed through her. "I think he should see a doctor. There may be medication to help him sleep or to cope with his depression. Could you make him go?"

"I can't make him do anything, but I strongly suggested that to him. It's good to see him out of bed and interested in working again, but he needs to work on healing spiritually as well as mentally and physically. He's not going to get that in a doctor's office. He needs his church."

She nodded. "I know. It's been so hard to get him motivated. I had hoped that, now that he's working, we could get back into a routine."

"It's up to you and your brother to make sure your father comes to church next Sunday," the bishop said. "He's aware of the consequences if he doesn't."

"What are the consequences?" she whispered.

"He will be shunned for six weeks. And if he confesses and repents at the end of that, all will be well."

"And if he doesn't?" she whispered.

The bishop put his hand on her arm. "He will."

"But if he doesn't?" Candace pressed.

"Then I will have no choice but to make it permanent."

10

Micah and Simon stayed with Lemuel after the bishop left and helped him cut out the wood for a new project. Betsy's future kitchen furniture was in various stages of completion, but Micah had suggested that Lemuel make something for Candace to remember her mother by. So they were making a garden bench.

When Lemuel was working, he seemed just fine. It was when he stopped that Micah could see the grief overtaking him again. Micah asked him questions whenever he saw that faraway look in Lemuel's eyes. But Micah was getting tired and hungry, and all three of them had a full day ahead of them tomorrow. They should all quit for the day.

"I should be going," Micah said. "Aenti Judy will be wondering where I am."

Lemuel was too engrossed in his work to respond.

"Daed," Simon said in a louder voice, "I'm going to drive Micah home. And I should see if Esther needs help with the Kinner."

"She's already in bed," Micah said. "Candace brought over some beef stew to Esther. She fed her and the kids and put them all to bed." He had gone to check on Candace an hour ago, and to grab a couple of sandwiches to tide them over until they could convince Lemuel to come in. The bishop's family had left shortly after he'd levied his ultimatum. Candace was understandably upset about the bishop telling her that Lemuel needed to go to church or he would be shunned.

Micah had tried to reassure her that they would do everything in their power to make that not happen. Bishop Mark wasn't trying to punish a grieving husband—he was trying to get Lemuel to accept the help of the congregation and the faith.

Unfortunately, Candace wasn't convinced. She had just come back from Esther's house, looking exhausted herself.

"I don't know what I'd do without my sister some days. I'll take care of the chores and call it a night." Simon rubbed his hand over his face. "Daed, Micah and I are going to go."

"I'm not ready to come in yet," Lemuel said.

Micah saw the pile of blankets and an old pillow in the corner of the workshop. He had a feeling that Lemuel had slept out here last night. Even with the small woodstove in the corner, it would have been a cold and uncomfortable situation. The sandwich Micah had brought back lay untouched on the workbench.

"Candace made some beef stew. Will you come in and have some?" Simon asked his father.

"Nee, I want to get some more work done on this. Have her bring me out a bowl."

"I think she's already in bed," Micah said. "She said she was heading there."

"Then I'll warm up some on the stove later," Lemuel said, still focused on his work.

"Are you sure, Daed?"

When Lemuel didn't answer him, Simon sighed. "I'll see you tomorrow, then."

As they left, Micah looked over his shoulder, but Lemuel didn't even acknowledge their absence. "I'm a little worried about him," Micah said as he climbed into Simon's buggy.

"He was worse," Simon said. "I'm glad the woodworking seems to be getting him more interested in the world again, but I wish his faith hadn't been so shaken by Mamm's death. It was too much to hope for that he would join us for the ice-skating party, but Esther and Candace thought it would be good for him to be with the community again."

"He just wasn't ready."

"I hope he took the bishop's words to heart. I know I'll do everything I can to make sure he's at work and at church."

"He has to want to do it for himself," Micah said. "For some reason, I think he's afraid to go to church, though I don't know why."

"Afraid?" Simon said. "I think he's more angry than anything else."

"Anger usually comes from a place of fear or unfairness. In this case, I think it's both. He feels it's unfair that his wife died so suddenly, and I think maybe he's afraid that Gött has stopped listening to his prayers."

Simon didn't reply, but gripped the reins tightly as they rode down the streets. A few cars passed by them, but for the most part, the night was quiet.

Finally, Simon broke the silence. "How do I help him?"

"I think your family is doing all it can. However, don't overlook yourselves. You are all still grieving and need to take time to come to terms with everything that's changed. You cannot focus so much on getting your father through his grief that you neglect your own healing. When my sister died, we went through the same thing. It takes a long time. Nothing will ever be normal as you remember it, but you'll find a new way to live."

Nodding, Simon steered the horse through the final turn to the Eichers' farm. "That makes a lot of sense. Did your bishop tell you that?"

"Nee, my Daed did. He would make a *gut* bishop when it's time to pick the next one in our community. Which may be soon. Our current bishop is getting on in years and his mind slips."

"I'm sorry to hear that. Is it Alzheimer's?"

"Ja."

Simon winced. "Terrible disease."

"Our minister and deacons have been taking on a lot more of our bishop's responsibility because he's been sick. It might not be long now."

"I'm sorry to hear about it."

"Me too. He's a *gut* man. Very wise, and skilled at tempering justice with kindness. It's sad. He forgets who and where he is sometimes. Other times, he's the same man I looked up to when I was a boy. I loved his sermons and valued his thoughts. It's so hard to see him fade away."

Simon sighed. "I can understand that. Have you ever thought about staying here?"

Micah was surprised by the change in subject, but didn't ask what had brought it on. "Nee, my Daed has some land for me, and while I'm not going to turn it into a tobacco farm, I have plans to build a workshop there."

"That's a shame," Simon said. "You're a *gut* man to have around. And my sister will miss you when you go."

Micah wanted to ask him why he thought Candace wouldn't go with him if he asked her, but it was far too soon for that. He had only been here a week and didn't want to presume too much. But it seemed that Simon could read minds—or maybe Micah's intentions had been a little obvious.

"Because," Simon continued as if Micah had asked after all, "she wouldn't want to leave my father all alone. And while he could always live with Esther and me, he wouldn't want to leave his home. At least not for a long while yet. He doesn't consider himself old enough for a *Dawdy Haus*."

That made sense. Candace was devoted to her family, which he admired. It was something to consider, but he was confident that there was a solution. It would just take some time and thought.

Simon pulled up in front of Aenti Judy's house and Micah hopped down. "Do you want to come in?"

"Nee, I've got Candace's beef stew and evening chores waiting for me at home. I'll see you tomorrow. Thanks again for all your help today."

"You're welcome. Please tell Esther it was a beautiful day and I think she's a wonderful hostess."

"She'll appreciate that." Simon waved as he pulled the buggy around. Micah waved back and went into the house.

Aenti Judy was knitting in her rocking chair by the fire. "How's Lemuel?"

"He's troubled. But Simon thinks it's better than it has been."

"Did he even come out to the pond?"

"Nee. He stayed in his workshop the entire day. He has a list of projects he wants to do, and that's been keeping his mind occupied."

"The community is worried about him."

"I think he's slowly coming around." Micah went into the kitchen to see if there were any leftovers from supper. The counters were wiped clean and everything was neat and tidy. He thought back on Candace's kitchen, which was not as organized, but there had been a plate of cookies and some bread out. He could almost taste her sourdough bread and goat cheese.

"The fried chicken is for your lunches tomorrow, but if you're hungry I can make you something."

"I can wait until breakfast," Micah said, pushing down a slight pang of hunger. He didn't want his Aenti to go to any trouble.

"Did you get a chance to skate with Betsy?" Judy asked.

"Ja," he said, not wanting to elaborate that it was mostly Amos who skated with Betsy.

"She'll make a good wife."

"I'm glad you think so." He would like to know why she wasn't encouraging Amos to court Betsy, but it was getting late and he needed to be rested for the day ahead. "I'm going to turn in. Good night."

The rest of the week was full of long hours and not much downtime, but Micah was enjoying keeping busy at the jobsite. Lemuel came to work every day and didn't mention last Sunday's conversation with Bishop Mark or the upcoming Sunday's church service. Micah went home with Lemuel every day, where they worked in the workshop until supper.

Candace was an excellent cook and always had new desserts for him to try, making sure he had a few treats to take home with him as well. It helped with the late-night snack addiction he seemed to be developing. After the meal, Micah worked with Lemuel on the bench, and by the end of the week, it was ready to be painted.

Thursday night, Lemuel had just sanded it down for the last time. "Do you think I should paint it white or leave just a coating of stain on it?"

They hadn't talked a lot about his wife or much of anything that wasn't related to the craft of woodworking or construction, but Micah thought this was as good an opening to do so as anything. "What would she have liked?"

Lemuel's face crumpled a bit. "I think she would have liked it white, so that she could spot it easier."

"We could also paint her name on it in her favorite color. What was it?"

"Violet."

"Is there a Bible verse she liked? We could paint that on it too."

Scowling, Lemuel stood up. "That'll do for now. Come on, I should be getting you home."

Micah set down the tool he'd been holding and then cleaned up his work area while Lemuel tapped his foot impatiently. "I've never been to the Stoltzfus farm," Micah said. "They're hosting the church service on Sunday. Maybe we could bring Sarah's bench and show the bishop what we've accomplished in a week."

"Is church this Sunday?" Lemuel asked.

Micah couldn't tell if he had genuinely forgotten or was deliberately playing dumb. "Yes. I know my Aenti is looking forward to seeing you. As is everyone else, I'm sure. But Judy always asks about you. One of these nights, you should come in for a cup of tea."

"After a long day, I'm not in the mood for visiting," he grumbled.

"I can understand that, but she's unbeatable in Rook. I was hoping someone could give her some competition in cards."

He snorted. "She always was a tough competitor. When her husband was alive, the four of us would play once a week."

"Maybe we can bring Candace with us one night next week and play."

Lemuel thought about it. "Maybe."

"What about me?" Candace came into the workshop with a couple of mugs and a carafe of hot cocoa.

"We were just calling it quits," Lemuel said.

"Then I came in just in time." She handed them each a mug and filled it with steaming chocolate. Even Lemuel couldn't resist after a small sip.

"What have you two been working on so hard this week?" she asked.

Micah gestured to the bench. "Your Daed made this in your Mamm's memory. We're going to paint it white and maybe put her name in violet on the front. Do you know of a small Bible verse or quote that she liked? We could paint it on the seat."

"I don't have a good enough hand to do something that detailed. It would ruin it." Lemuel took a long drink of his cocoa.

"Esther could do it," Candace said, eyes brimming. "And I know just the verse. Isaiah 41:10. 'Fear not, for I am with you. Be not dismayed, for I *am* your God.'"

"'I will strengthen you, yes, I will help you. I will uphold you with My righteous right hand,'" Micah finished for her.

She beamed, and he found himself smiling back. He wished they could spend an hour or so playing a board game or just chatting. If the weather was nicer, they could sit out on the porch and talk without anyone raising an eyebrow.

"That's a little long to paint on a bench seat," Lemuel grumbled.

"Which one do you like then, Daed?" Candace asked.

"I'll think about it." He drained his mug and handed it back to her. "I'll meet you up front, Micah."

Micah watched him leave, unease filling him.

"It's a beautiful bench," she said.

"He's a skilled craftsman. I'm learning a lot from him. How has he been when I'm not here?"

She topped off his cup. "It depends. Sometimes, he stays out here and works until I tell him the light from his workshop is keeping me up. Others, he goes straight to bed. He doesn't talk much, but he's been more active. He finishes his chores before going to work in the morning. I can't complain." Candace sighed. "Still, I wish he found some joy or peace in what he's doing."

"That'll come," Micah said, laying a comforting hand on her shoulder.

"I'm glad you're here." Tears brimmed in her beautiful eyes.

He could stand anything but her grief. "Don't cry. It will be all right. I promise."

"How can you promise that?"

"Because I have faith."

She gazed in the direction her father had gone. "Faith is hard sometimes."

"It is." They walked back to the house, their shoulders brushing.

Friday was payday and everyone's spirits were high. They'd all worked two long weeks, and the paychecks would go a long way to feeding their families and catching up on bills.

Micah was reinforcing a wall at the jobsite when he heard the police sirens. At first, he didn't think anything of it, but then they got louder and there was a commotion in the front of the building.

It wasn't his break, so he didn't feel comfortable stopping work. His cousins continued pounding nails and sawing wood. He could hear the crackle of radios and the sound of running feet. Micah got a bad feeling in his stomach and carefully put down his tools. Following the noise, he saw an ambulance out front. As he was gawking at it, a team of EMTs ran out alongside a stretcher.

Simon was with them, his eyes wide and panicked.

Micah focused on the stretcher. His heart bucked as he looked at the figure lying there.

It was Lemuel.

"What happened?" Micah called as they passed him.

"Tell Esther and Candace there has been an accident."

Micah followed them out to the ambulance. "Which hospital?" His heart thundered in his chest. Poor Simon looked out of his mind with fear.

"First General on Main Street," the EMT answered him.

They bundled into the ambulance, and it wailed away.

How could he tell Candace?

11

Candace hummed as she sorted recipes on the dining room table. She had made a pot of tea, and Betsy had brought over a tray of crustless tea sandwiches so they could have a grown-up tea party. Esther had arrived with cinnamon raisin scones. It was a rare event when both Betsy and Candace had the day off from the store. The men were at work and Abraham was napping in the living room in the crib his Grossdaedi had made.

Betsy fed a sheet of paper into the typewriter and paused, her fingers hovering over the keys. "We need a name for the cookbook."

Esther paced, rubbing her back and wincing. The larger her belly grew, the harder it was for her to find comfort in any position. "What about Sarah's Sweets?"

"The recipes are not all sweet, though," Candace pointed out.

"Beacheys' Best?" Betsy suggested.

Candace beamed. "I like that. And underneath it we can put a subtitle. How about 'Amish experiments in cooking'?"

"Do we want to say experiments?" Esther asked. "That sounds like we aren't sure they were a success."

"That's a good point." Candace poured herself some more tea and allowed herself to wish that her mother were there to help them. Of course, Mamm would have thought it was foolish to make a book of her favorite recipes. "But we want to stand out from the other Amish cookbooks out there."

"How about 'A Month of Amish Meals' for the subtitle?" Betsy asked. "We could have a page with what they could make for breakfast, lunch, and supper, and then have the recipes follow that."

"I like that," Esther said.

"Okay, then we should separate these into breakfast, lunch, and supper recipes." Candace started making three piles.

"And if we run short on recipes, we can fill in with non-food recipes. Like your soap and lotions. And some other crafts," Betsy said.

"This is going to be a good book," Esther said. "Once it's all typed up, you can hire an Englisch printer to make the booklets for you."

"Karen has already said she would let me sell it in the store by the soaps and lotions."

"That reminds me," Esther said. "I should crochet some more washcloths to sell. It'll give me something to do while I'm waiting for this baby to come."

"You can use some of Mamm's cotton yarn. It's in the cedar chest along with her hooks and needles. I'll get it."

"Nonsense. I'm not an invalid." Esther walked over to the wooden chest and winced as she bent to open the hinged lid. She shuffled through it for a moment, then came up with a cone of peach-and-white cotton yarn. "Here we are."

Candace wrinkled her nose at the color. "I liked the blue-and-white yarn better, but that was a dollar more. Mamm liked her bargains."

They all looked up when a car sped up their driveway. All three of them stepped out on the porch when it screeched to a stop and the passenger door burst open.

"Micah," Candace gasped.

He stumbled out of the car and staggered toward them with his hat in his hand, visibly shaken. His face was drawn and pale, and Candace suddenly found herself dreading what he would say.

"Candace, your Daed is in the hospital. There was an accident."

"Accident?" She gripped his arm. "What happened?"

"I don't know exactly. I didn't see it, but the foreman said a wall collapsed on him."

Esther gasped and swayed. Betsy caught her and helped her inside.

"I'll be right back," Micah called to the driver of the car.

Before she knew what he was doing, he hooked an arm around her waist and led her into the house. She realized she was numb and her legs were shaky. She was grateful for the support and clung to him. This couldn't be happening. She couldn't lose her Daed too. "Is he all right?"

"I don't know. He wasn't conscious when I saw him taken out on a stretcher. Simon is with him. He wanted me to come and get you. Grab your things. It's a two-hour ride. They took him to the hospital closest to the jobsite."

"I should go too," Esther fretted.

"Nee," Candace said. "Stay here. I'll send Simon home. Betsy, can you stay with her until Simon arrives?" Candace grabbed her coat off the rack and her large tote bag where she kept her wallet.

"I'm fine," Esther said, stuffing the cone and a crochet hook into Candace's bag. "You'll be doing a lot of waiting in the hospital. This will help keep you busy."

"I had planned on staying all day anyway," Betsy said. "We can arrange the recipes and maybe test some out so there's something to eat when you get back."

Candace squeezed her friend's arm gratefully. "I'll send word if I can. If not, Simon will give you the details. Expect him back at the normal time. I'll make sure he's on the van."

Abraham started to wake up from his nap with a sulky wail. Candace knew if she didn't leave right away, she would start crying with him. She faced Micah, who wrapped his arm around her again and helped her to the car.

"What if he's . . ." Candace couldn't say the word.

"Don't think that." Micah settled her into the car, tucking her long black dress in so he wouldn't shut it in the door. He ran around to the other side of the car and got in. "Are you all right to drive back?" he asked the driver.

"No problem. I used to be a truck driver. I'm used to the long haul. But I will need to stop for coffee and gas when we get about halfway there."

"Denki—thank you. I really appreciate it."

"Yes," Candace managed to find her voice again. "Thank you."

The driver nodded and pulled out of her driveway. Candace tried to give a comforting wave to her friend and sister-in-law but she wasn't sure she was convincing.

"He's in the best place he could be right now. I'm sure they're doing everything possible to help him."

"It's not fair that he was injured like this," Candace said. "He was doing so much better. I'm so afraid this will set him back."

Micah reached over and grabbed her hand. "I know you are."

"Tell me again what the foreman told you."

Closing his eyes, Micah took a deep breath. She realized this situation must be nearly as traumatizing for him as it was for her. "It all went so fast. The sirens, the ambulance. Lou was worried. He had cleared the area when I went back there."

"You went to where a wall fell on my Daed? Micah, you could have been hurt."

"I was careful." He squeezed her hand. "There was a lot of drywall and wires, but none of them were live. A few beams were on the floor. Debris was all over the place. The stories were confusing. Someone said he used a sawhorse as a stepladder, lost his balance, and crashed into the wall, taking it down with him. But another person said the wall had been shaky and fell on Lemuel when he was moving his sawhorse and banged into it."

"What really happened? Someone's not telling the truth."

"I'm not sure. It could be that they both thought that's what they saw, but it could be something else entirely. All we know for certain is they had to pull him out from under the wall."

"Gött have mercy," she whispered.

"You know he's stubborn and tough. He'll fight."

She whispered her greatest fear. "What if he doesn't want to? He was so broken about Mamm. What if he decides to let go and be with her?"

"I'm not sure that's his decision to make. Gött is watching over him."

"What if he hit his head? Or broke a bone?"

"Then he'll stay in the hospital a few days until he heals. After that, it depends on what the doctors say."

"Thank you for coming and getting me." Candace felt dizzy. She forced herself to take deep breaths to calm down. She had to be the strong one. Again. She needed to hold it together so Simon would feel comfortable going home to Esther, who needed him there. She could stay with her father.

"If it were up to me, I wouldn't have contacted you."

Candace couldn't believe what she was hearing. "Why not?"

"This was your day off. There's nothing you can do at the hospital. I wish you could have had more time doing something you liked with your friends."

"Micah, I would have felt so guilty about having a pleasant time while my brother worried and my father was in the hospital."

"You have nothing to feel guilty about."

She blew out a sigh. "I do feel guilty though. Part of me thinks I shouldn't have pushed him to go back to work so soon. The other part is punishing me for not forcing him to go talk to someone sooner. If not the bishop, maybe Judy, or even a doctor."

"None of this is your fault. You have been helping your family in the best way you know how."

"It's been so hard." Candace sighed and closed her eyes. Climbing into her bed for a few months was starting to sound more and more attractive. But she realized that she would feel just as guilty if she did that as she would if she had spent the day enjoying herself while her brother and father were in the hospital.

She wondered what her Mamm would do in this situation. First of all, she'd tell her to stop holding Micah's hand. Reluctantly, she released it and kept her hand on her lap. It had felt good to lean on him and accept his comfort. But it wasn't proper.

Then, her Mamm would make sure she had all the facts before reacting with emotion. Mamm wouldn't worry until she knew exactly what was going on, so that's what Candace would do. And when she thought that, she no longer felt her mother was gone forever. Mamm would always be with her in moments like this. Her teaching would always be a source of strength for Candace. All Candace had to do to stay close to her Mamm was to keep her memory alive in her heart.

Straightening her shoulders, she felt a missing piece of herself come back and settle. It was then she realized that her family would be all right. They would handle this latest disaster as they did all things—with faith in Gött and their family.

When they got to the hospital, Simon was slumped in the waiting room chair. He got up when she rushed toward him.

"How is he?" Candace asked him.

"He fractured two ribs and has a concussion, but he's going to be fine."

She sagged, and if Micah was right behind her to hold her up, she didn't think that was improper. "Can I see him?"

"The doctor is in there now. Daed wants to sleep because he's in such pain, but they have to keep waking him up to check on him."

"Can't they give him something for the pain?"

"Not with the concussion. They want to keep him for a few days and then move him down to a convalescent rehabilitation center closer to Randolph."

"I brought the checkbook. Where do I go to put a payment down?" she asked. This could very well bankrupt them, but she would worry about that later.

"Hold off on that for now. Lou said he's probably covered under the workman's compensation policy the Mennonite firm has."

"What do you mean?"

"It means the bill may be paid in part or maybe even in full by their insurance."

Her knees wobbled, and this time Micah helped her to a seat. "How can that be possible?"

"From what Lou was telling me, in order to bid on this job, it was required not only to have a valid contractor's license, but enough insurance to cover any on-the-job injuries."

If that wasn't her Mamm looking out for her family, Candace didn't know what was. "I'll be right back," she said. She headed to the ladies' room where she could cry in relief without causing a scene. Her father would live. And she wouldn't have to plead to the bishop for financial help just when her father seemed to be rejecting his faith and community.

When she had composed herself, she splashed cold water on her face and patted it dry with a paper towel. Micah and Simon were standing by the coffee vending machine talking in lowered voices. They cut off their conversation when she came up to them, which made her suspicious.

"What are you two up to?" She narrowed her eyes at them.

"You can go in and see Daed," Simon said, avoiding the question. "This way." They left the waiting area and walked down the long corridor, past several patients' rooms. "Don't get upset when you see him. They have him hooked up to several machines that are monitoring his heart and vitals. It looks scary, but he's okay."

Swallowing hard, she nodded. Micah opened the door for them. Candace was glad Simon had warned her. Her Daed looked so frail in the hospital bed and there were ugly purple bruises covering half his face.

"Daed?" she whispered.

"He's probably out. Let him sleep," Simon said. "The nurses will wake him soon for tests and medicine anyway."

"I'll stay with him," she said. "Why don't you see if you can still catch the van home? Esther will need you tonight."

"What about you? How are you getting home?"

"I'll stay here."

"They'll kick you out at eleven when visiting hours close."

She blinked. "I'm sure I can get them to let me stay. I can sleep in the chair."

"Nee," Simon said kindly. "We'll both stay here and then hire a car to take us home. Then we'll bring another car up to visit him tomorrow."

"What if he wakes up in the middle of the night? He'll be all alone. I'm staying," she said firmly.

Micah and Simon exchanged a look.

"You need to go home to Esther," Micah told Simon. "I can stay here, and if they do make her leave, I'll hire a car and bring her home. If they let us stay, I can sleep on the waiting room couch."

"Micah, you don't have to," she protested.

"Simon needs to get home. I don't have anywhere to be. And I'd like to help Lemuel. He wouldn't want you to be here all alone."

Candace bit her lip. "Well, if you're sure."

"I am. Simon and I will figure out the details while you sit with your Daed. We'll be back."

Nodding, she pulled the padded chair up close to the hospital bed and just watched her father's chest rise and fall. She didn't understand what most of the monitors said, but the rhythm and beeping was oddly soothing, even if the lights in the room were too bright. She dug around in her purse until she found her prayer book. Candace read to him, hoping it comforted him as much as it did her.

The nurse came in and woke him to check his vital signs and his pupils. Candace didn't like to see the pain in her father's eyes.

"I was trying to sleep," he grumbled.

The fact that he was grumpy actually made Candace feel better.

"You took a big hit in the head, Mr. Beachey, and you have a concussion. It's not going to be a restful twenty-four hours for you."

"My chest hurts."

"You've fractured a few ribs. That's going to take some time to heal."

"It's hard to breathe. I don't like all these tubes attached to me."

"I'm sorry, but they have to stay in for a while. If you rest when you can and keep the IV and oxygen lines in, this ordeal will be over sooner. And then you can go home."

"Why are you here?" he barked at Candace.

"Simon had to go back home to Esther," she said simply.

The nurse left and Micah came in.

"Is something wrong with Esther?" her father asked.

"Nee, she's fine. I just didn't want her to be alone with the Kinner."

Her father nodded. "Micah, is everything all right at the job?"

"Ja, things are *gut*." Micah leaned against the wall with his hands in his pockets. "Do you remember what happened?"

He frowned. "I needed to check the molding on the ceiling. I climbed up to see it better and I guess I lost my balance."

"You should have used a stepladder," Candace scolded.

"Why? I had a sawhorse."

Micah put a hand over his mouth, but the crinkling of his eyes told Candace he was grinning. "You don't have to worry about anything," he said when he'd composed himself. "Lou's insurance will cover your medical bills and the rest of us will get the job done."

"I'll be back to work in a few days."

Shaking his head, Micah said, "I'm not a doctor, but I don't think it's going to be that quick."

Her father sighed. "Take my daughter home, Micah. I need my rest and her yammering bothers me."

Candace blinked back tears. "I'll be quiet, Daed."

"Go home."

Candace wanted to argue, but Micah said, "Let him get some rest. We will check on him tomorrow."

"Are you sure, Daed?"

But he didn't answer her. His eyes were closed, and if he wasn't asleep, he was doing a good job of pretending he was.

Micah asked one of the people in the waiting room to call a cab for them. As they waited outside for it, he took her hand and she was so distraught, she let him. There were so many people around, it couldn't be scandalous.

"Don't let anything your father said back there bother you. He's hurting and lashing out."

"I wouldn't have bothered him," she said, hearing her voice shake and hating it. "I would have prayed in my mind so he didn't hear me."

"I think he was embarrassed that he caused the accident by not using the stepladder. That and the pain have made him surly. It has nothing to do with you."

"I shouldn't have said those things to him," she fretted.

"He needed to hear them. He's not a child. He can take some hard truths."

"It's just that he's seemed so fragile lately." Candace climbed into the cab when it pulled up outside of the hospital.

Micah gave the driver an address that was unfamiliar to her.

"Where are we going?"

"To the jobsite. If you don't mind waiting an hour or so, we can take the van back home."

"Nee," she said. "I don't mind."

When they reached the site, Micah went back to work. Simon was also busy, trying to make up for lost time. She found a seat and pulled out the hook and yarn that Esther had stuffed in her bag. It wasn't how she had planned her day off, but crocheting a washcloth worked wonders for her mental state. It was a mindless pattern, yet she felt as if she'd accomplished something when it was done.

Her father was all right. The hospital bill would be paid. They had survived one more thing.

12

While Lemuel was in the hospital, Micah and Simon worked out a routine. Simon would help Candace with the morning chores, and Amos and Micah helped with the evening chores in exchange for supper. It worked out well for everyone. Judy had fewer mouths to feed. Candace wasn't overworked, and Betsy came over after supper every night to join them playing cards or a board game, so Amos was happy as well.

"How's your Daed doing?" Micah asked over his third helping of chicken pot pie. It was one of the recipes that Candace had found in her mother's things. She was cooking them herself so she could understand what needed to go in the cookbook she was putting together.

"They're moving him to the convalescent center just a few miles from here tomorrow," she said. "He hates the physical therapy, but it's helping him get stronger. He was having trouble breathing, but it's better now. We've been blessed. He may think he's done with Gött, but Gött certainly isn't done with him."

Micah did miss his woodworking lessons, but he was enjoying the quiet evenings with his friends. In just a few short days, he could see a change in Candace. She was less stressed and anxious. She smiled more and had an air of serenity around her that enchanted him.

He was falling for her fast, and he hoped with all his might that she was feeling the same.

"Judy has been visiting as often as she can get a ride, and I think it's helped his recovery."

"Mamm's not a nurse," Amos said.

"Nee, but she is good company. I've walked in on them bickering like an old married couple, and then again while they're playing cards. Sometimes they're both just sitting there, Judy knitting and Daed reading the paper." Candace smiled wistfully. "I think he's missed that type of routine, that camaraderie. And it's easier to adjust to when he's not home with all his memories. In a strange way, I think the wall falling on him healed him more than hurt him."

"I don't know about that," Micah said. "Busted ribs hurt a ton. I cracked a rib once and all I wanted to do was lie in bed. Even breathing hurt. But it healed in time. Every now and then I still get a twinge."

"It's like grief in a way," Candace said.

Micah nodded. "I can see that. You're never quite the same again, but you go on."

They finished their food in a comfortable silence. Esther brought over an apple strudel for dessert and chaperoned them from the living room, knitting by the fire. Most nights she snoozed on the couch, and Betsy gave them all a ride home when they left. Sometimes Simon would come over instead and join them for a game. That was more likely on the nights when Candace was testing her Mamm's dessert recipes.

They heard a buggy approaching, and Amos perked up. That would be Betsy. Amos had confirmed what Candace had said about Betsy not wanting to go into business with her sister in Pennsylvania. Betsy also didn't want to own her own bakery. She was content to bake for the Amish Market part-time and spend the rest of her time at home. But in that case, Micah wasn't sure what the bishop had against Amos. Maybe he simply didn't know his daughter's heart at all.

Candace cleared the supper plates from the table to give them room to put the board game down. They were going to try a new one tonight and Amos had spent the last half hour reading the rules and probably memorizing them.

"Hello," Betsy said from the door, which was odd since she usually just walked in.

Frowning, Candace got up and went over to see what was going on. "Oh," she said. "Please come in, Bishop Mark."

Amos winced and Micah swallowed a groan.

"We were hoping not to disturb your supper."

"We just finished, but you're welcome to join us for some apple strudel and coffee."

"That's most gracious of you."

Micah stiffened at the new voice. It couldn't be. He half rose out of his seat as his father trailed in behind the bishop. "Daed?"

Candace whirled to look at him.

"Micah," he said with a smile. "I wanted to surprise you."

"You did," Micah said, shaking his hand. "Is Mamm with you?"

"She didn't want to take the car trip in this weather. She was afraid the car would break down."

Candace recovered herself admirably. "Please have a seat. I'm Candace Beachey, and that's my sister-in-law, Esther."

Esther had roused herself and come into the dining room. "It's a pleasure to meet a part of Micah's family."

"Hello, Onkel Ezekiel," Amos said, rising from the table.

"Amos. You've gotten so tall." They shook hands, and then everyone sat back down while Esther and Candace went into the kitchen. After a few minutes of awkward silence, Candace came back into the dining room and passed out mugs of coffee.

"Well," Micah's Daed said. "I've spoken with your father, Betsy, and he has agreed to have you come to Pennsylvania to your sister. You can ride with Micah once his carpenter job is over."

"That won't be until probably April," Micah said hurriedly.

Ezekiel frowned. "You said March."

"Well, that was before. We're short a man now."

"Ja," Bishop Mark said, turning to Candace who had just sat down. "I'm looking forward to visiting your father at the rehabilitation center this week. Do you know when he'll be allowed home?"

"It depends on the progress he makes in physical therapy. He's having some movement issues, but probably in a few weeks."

"You'll let him know we're all praying for him," the bishop said.

"I will. That will mean a lot to him."

Esther asked the question Micah hadn't known how to voice. "So, Mr. Zehr, how long are you planning to stay in Randolph?"

"Well, I know my son is working long hours, but I wanted to get a visit in with him and maybe join in the sugaring. My sister-in-law tells me they have just tapped the trees."

Two whole weeks. At least. Longer if the sap ran slower. Micah stifled a groan.

"Are you staying with the Eichers?" Candace asked, her eyes downcast as she played with her strudel instead of eating it.

"Nee, the bishop was kind enough to offer his home, since we're practically family."

Micah stared helplessly into his strudel. This was all his fault. He should have written home to his father and said that his eye was on Candace and not Betsy. He'd honestly thought there would be more time for that. After all, his carpentry job wasn't anywhere near ending.

"I'm looking forward to getting to know you," Betsy said meekly.

Candace shot her an incredulous look before lowering her eyes again. Although she couldn't blame Betsy. She'd had to say *something*.

They finished dessert with stilted and awkward conversation. Ezekiel and Bishop Mark didn't seem to notice anything was amiss.

"The apple strudel was delicious," the bishop said.

"Denki," Esther said.

"We are going to head back for an early night," the bishop said. "The rest of you can join us so Candace doesn't have to hitch up the buggy."

Not really having a choice, they agreed. Micah wanted to linger and explain to Candace that he wasn't sure what was going on, but he didn't get the chance.

They dropped Esther back home first and when they arrived at the Eichers' farm, Amos hurried out of the buggy with a terse, "*Gut'n Owed*, everyone."

Micah would have followed, but decided he wouldn't get a decent night's sleep if he didn't speak with his Daed. "I'll ride back with you. I wanted to have a few moments to talk with my father. Then I'll walk home. It's a nice enough night."

The bishop and Ezekiel exchanged a look and shrug. "Whatever you want."

Betsy looked up at him with wide eyes.

He still wasn't sure what was going on with that, but he did know that he couldn't put off his conversation with his father any longer. When they arrived back at the Miller farm, Betsy and her father went inside while Micah and his father went to the barn to put away the horse and buggy.

"Your friends seem nice," Ezekiel said. "And Betsy is a lovely girl."

"She is," Micah said, longing to say that it was Candace he was interested in, no matter how nice Betsy was. But between his father staying at the bishop's house and Betsy giving him strange looks, he didn't want to broach the subject before he had more information.

"What did you want to talk to me about? Can't we do this inside where it's warmer?"

Micah shook himself out of his reverie. "I have something to tell you and you're not going to like it."

Ezekiel folded his arms across his chest.

"I want to talk to you about my job. You know that I have been enjoying my time working in the carpentry crew."

His father nodded impatiently, clearly waiting for him to get to the point.

"And after work, I've been apprenticing with Lemuel Beachey—that's Candace's father—in his workshop. I'm learning new wood techniques and he's going to teach me cabinetry."

"Ja, I know. That's all been in your letters. Get to the part that I'm not going to like."

Micah took a deep breath. "Daed, I don't want to be a farmer. I never did, and you know that. But I want to make sure you understand. I will not be growing alfalfa, tobacco, hay, or any cash crop on my farm. I'll have a small garden, but just enough for my family. I don't want to have a dairy farm or give farm tours to Englischers." He paused to see his father's reaction and was slightly buoyed when there wasn't one.

"I see that you've given this some thought. And what do you plan to do with my land?"

Breaking out into a big grin, Micah said, "I'm going to open a cabinet shop. I want to specialize in kitchen cabinets. I'm getting a lot of practice in with Lemuel, and I like my day job. Working with wood and building things is what I want to do with my life."

"I see," his father said again. He rocked back on his heels. "You were right. I don't like it."

"I'm sorry," Micah said. "I wish I could be what you want me to be. But I'm not a farmer and I never will be."

"That, of course, is your decision. You are an adult. However, my decision is to not give you the land if you're not going to farm it."

Micah wasn't sure he heard him right. "But where am I going to build my house?"

"I'm sure once you and your bride come to live with us, it's only a matter of time before she convinces you that you need your own home. And you know that the only way to get those acres will be to use it as farmland."

"Why are you doing this?" Micah asked, stunned by his father's words.

Ezekiel clapped a hand on his shoulder. "You are my son, and there will always be a place for you in my home. But if you want this workshop, you will have to save up and buy the land for it yourself. My land is too valuable to give away as anything else but for farms that will sustain our way of life."

Micah didn't know what to say. He gaped at his father.

"Now, I'm going inside to warm up. You can join me and perhaps tell your bride-to-be about our conversation. Maybe she can talk some sense into you. Or you can walk off your temper to your Aenti's house and we can discuss this again when you're in a more reasonable mood."

Before Micah could protest, Ezekiel turned and stalked away.

Micah stood, stunned. His world had just tilted on its axis. What was he going to do? He realized that while he didn't come to Randolph looking for someone to spend his life with, he had found her. He wondered if she felt the same. He thought about their shared glances and how well they got along whether it was working on a crossword puzzle or just talking.

But what girl wanted to get married and not have a house of her own? He wanted to give her that new home and a new start where she didn't have to work at an Englisch market if she didn't want to. Would she even want to leave Randolph and her family to live with his parents and their overwhelming disappointment in him? Would she grow to resent him, having the temptation of the farmland in their grasp, if only Micah would give in to the inevitable and become a farmer?

Micah trudged through the cow pasture to his aunt's home. The lights were all out when he got there, so he went straight up to bed. However, as he stared up at the ceiling, he realized he had more questions than answers, and sleep was hard to come by.

13

Candace had asked Karen to cut her hours down to part-time while her father was sick. While Karen wasn't happy about it, she obliged. Candace did the chores at her farm, but stayed with Esther and Simon and helped there as well. It worked out for both of them because Esther needed more help in the mornings now that her due date was getting closer. On the days Candace had to work mornings at the Amish Market, she made breakfast the night before and packed Simon's and Gabriel's lunches. When she came back from work in the afternoon, she picked up Esther and her nephews so they could go visit her father.

Lemuel was ready to go home, but his body had other plans. There weren't any complications from the concussion, but he was having a hard time walking without pain from his ribs.

Today, she had to work in the afternoon, so she took Esther in to see him as soon as the convalescent home opened. Abraham was with them, even though Esther had wanted to see if Betsy could watch him until they got back. But because of her schedule change, Candace hadn't been working the same shifts as Betsy, so she hadn't been able to ask.

And anyway, she was waiting for either her or Micah to explain what was going on.

Micah had stopped coming over since Candace was basically living at Simon's house now. And Betsy hadn't visited either. It made Candace sad, and she missed her friends, but mostly she was confused.

What was going on? It wasn't as if she'd moved far away. They knew where she was. Why didn't they come to visit her anymore?

"Can I go home today?" her father grumbled.

"Nee, they're still worried that you'll catch pneumonia, since it's winter and your immune system is weak," Esther said. "You're looking to get out of here the first week of March. Don't pick him up!" Abraham was trying to climb up on the bed and Daed had reached to lift him up.

Spring, Candace thought wistfully. She moved from looking out the window to hoist Abraham up on top of the bed with his Grossdaedi.

"I'm breathing fine." He took several deep breaths that rattled and wheezed. "See?"

"That sounds awful," Esther informed him.

"Nonsense. My breathing has always sounded like that. I'll pick up my grandson whenever I want."

"Daed, please don't strain yourself," Candace said. "The doctor said your movement is limited and she wants you to work more on regaining mobility."

"Why? By the time they let me out of here, the carpentry job will be over. If I can get out of here now, I can at least hammer a nail and use the saw."

Not this again. Candace grasped her patience and said, "Daed, you can't even lift your arms over your head."

He glared at her.

"If you work on your therapy, by March you'll be able to do everything you've done before. But it's going to take a little more time. We all have our work. The men are to work on the jobsite, Esther and I are to work at home, and you are to work on getting better."

"And you're still going to be sore when you're discharged." Esther winced as she sat down. She was very pale.

"Do you want some water?" Candace asked.

She shook her head. "Nee, I'm fine. I'm just dizzy and out of breath all of a sudden."

Candace thought being dizzy and out of breath did not sound "fine." "All right, but please let me know if you need anything."

"I just need to sit for a bit. Keep an eye on Abraham. I don't want him crawling all over his Grossdaedi and accidentally putting a knee in his ribs or something."

"The boy is fine," her father grumbled, tousling Abraham's hair.

"Is Judy coming to visit today?" Candace asked.

"Probably. She's here every day. I'm surprised she doesn't have anything better to do."

Candace frowned. "Is she bothering you? I could ask her not to visit so much."

"Nee, she's fine," he said. "She's looking for a new husband and she thinks I'm it."

Esther and Candace stared at him in shock. Candace found her voice first. "I'm sure that's not the case. She knows that we're all still grieving Mamm's loss."

"Of course she does. We talk about your Mamm all the time."

That surprised her, but she was glad he was finally opening up. Still, the marriage thing haunted her. She wasn't sure she wanted Judy taking their mother's place. On the other hand, it might make her father less grief-stricken. "What do you think about that?" she asked carefully.

"About what?"

Candace almost ground her teeth in frustration. "Do you want to remarry?"

"I can't even get out of bed without assistance," he snapped. "How could I take care of a wife?"

"I meant when you heal."

"Ask me then."

Time, she thought. That was what they all needed. They all just needed to hang on until better weather, and then the garden and tourists would keep them busy so they could concentrate on something other than what was different in their lives now compared to how it had been when her mother was alive.

"How's your job going?" he asked her, his tone calmer.

"Fine. Karen has me on the registers more often than back in the bakery. She's given Mary more hours, so Betsy and Mary are working together more. I hate being up front, but I do get to see everyone in the community. And they're all asking about you and hoping you get better soon. You are in all their prayers."

"Fat lot of good that does."

"Daed," she said, warningly, "you can't talk like that. Not in front of Abraham anyway."

"Not in front of anyone," Esther said. "Has Bishop Mark come up to see you yet?"

Lemuel grunted as he shifted in bed. "Nee."

"He will." Esther wagged her finger at him. "And I want you to tell him everything. He's a wise man and he can help you work through this crisis of faith."

They visited for a couple more hours and then it was time to go so Candace could get to work on time. She took back the library books he was finished with and left with a list of subjects he wanted to read up on. It would be nice to spend a few hours in the library, but that would have to wait until tomorrow morning.

"I wish my Mamm was here," Esther said when they got back in the buggy.

"Me too." Candace sighed.

Esther squeezed her arm. "I'm sorry. That was thoughtless. At least mine is only in Indiana."

"It's all right. I knew what you meant. She'll come up after the Boppli is born, though, right?"

"Ja, but she gets carsick. She might take a train for most of the journey." Esther wrapped her arms around herself.

"Are you cold? There's a blanket in the back."

"Abraham's using it," Esther said, looking over her shoulder. "I'll be fine, but could you not drop me off at home? I don't want to be alone today."

Candace looked at her closely. "Are you all right? Is the Boppli coming?"

"I don't know. It could be just nerves."

"Do you want me to take you to your doctor?"

"Nee, I'm not having contractions or anything like that. I just want someone to talk to."

Candace could relate. "I could bring you down to the quilt store. You could look at the fabrics, and sit and talk with the quilters. I'm sure one of them will bring you home before Gabriel comes back from school."

"I'm not sure if I feel *that* social." Esther smiled. "Why don't you take me over to Judy Eicher's house? She's alone too, and I can stay with her until Simon comes home. If she wants to go visit your Daed, I can go with her. We can pick up Gabriel after school."

"That sounds like a good idea. But do me a favor. If she mentions Amos asking me to step out, don't encourage her."

"Even if Betsy and Micah are engaged?"

Her stomach twisted at the idea. "I don't know what's going on with that whole thing. I need to speak with Betsy when her parents aren't around. I haven't seen Micah since the night his Daed arrived."

"I'm sure things will work out. They have a way of doing that. Micah is probably catching up on his chores."

Candace had her doubts. She dropped off her sister-in-law at the Eichers', where Judy was thrilled for the company. Candace was early for work, but she saw Betsy's buggy so she went in anyway, hoping for a chance to talk with her.

"I'm so glad you're here," Karen said the moment she stepped in the store. "Go punch in and head for the bakery. Betsy will be back to help when she's finished her lunch. Mary is sick with the flu."

"Oh no." Candace hoped that she wouldn't catch it as well. All she needed was to be sick. Or worse, make her father or Esther sick. Washing her hands thoroughly, she put on her work apron and glanced at the display case. They were definitely low on the basics.

She saw that Betsy had several bowls of bread dough waiting to be punched down. The oven timer went off, and Candace turned to remove two trays of dinner rolls.

Betsy came running in from the break room. "You're here!"

"Ja, but go finish your lunch. I'll get some molasses cookies in the oven."

"There are a few logs of sugar cookie dough in the refrigerator, if you feel like rolling them out and using the Valentine's Day cookie cutters on them. I'll make pink icing when I get back."

Valentine's Day was Friday. She had almost forgotten.

Candace decided she would make some marshmallow fudge at home and bring it into the convalescent home for the nurses. Her Daed hated chocolate, so she made a mental note to make him some rice cereal treats. The Amish market was running a special on cereal and marshmallows this week.

She wondered if Micah liked chocolate. If she were stepping out with him, she would make him a cherry fry pie for the holiday. Maybe she would do it anyway. She'd have to make a bunch, though, and bring them over to the Eichers' farm. But that was all right. Judy visited her father most days and kept him occupied, playing cards and chatting.

Money was tight, though. Without her father's paycheck, it was just her part-time pay and what little Simon could afford out of his own budget for food. She would have to get creative and raid the clearance sections. That was the good thing about working here. She would get first crack at the deals, in addition to her employee discount.

Betsy came back from lunch just as the cookies went into the oven. "Denki, I was feeling a little overwhelmed. How's your Daed?"

Candace pulled a bowl toward her and punched down the bread. "He's frustrated that he can't go back to the carpentry job with Simon right away. It's going to be a long month."

"Are you coming to the sugaring this weekend or do you have to work?" They were expecting a hard freeze on Friday night, and then it was predicted that the temperature was going to fly up into the forties. Those sap buckets would be overflowing if the Eichers weren't quick about emptying them.

"I'm working in the morning, but I'll stop by afterward and see if I can help with the buckets. Esther's in charge of the pancakes."

Betsy smiled. "I can't wait for the first taste. I love the smell of the sugar shack. And maybe on Monday we can make some maple-glazed doughnuts."

Candace grinned. "We'll sell out faster than we can get them out of the oven."

"That's true. I'll eat five myself."

They worked together getting the bread and cookies in the oven and starting on dinner rolls. There were a few customers, but for the most part they could concentrate on baking. When they were mostly caught up, Candace figured now was as good a time as any to ask her friend the questions that had plagued her.

"So how has it been with Micah's Daed living with you? And what's all the marriage talk about?" Candace asked, taking out her frustrations on the bread dough.

Betsy grimaced. "It's been so awkward. Apparently Susan has been matchmaking down in Pennsylvania. She had convinced Micah's parents that I was desperate to go down there and start a bakery with her."

"More like you're desperate not to."

"Exactly. Did anyone think to ask me what I want? Or what Micah wants? I should have stood up and told them that night, but I was a little intimidated. I figured I'd be a coward and let Micah tell his Daed that he'd rather marry you instead."

Candace gasped. "Do you really think so?"

Betsy snorted. "I have eyes."

Candace's heart soared for a brief moment. Betsy wasn't wrong about things like that. She shoved her heart back into place and asked, in what she hoped was a casual tone, "So why didn't he?"

"He was probably as blindsided as I was. He's been over for dinner every night this week, and his father won't let him get a word in edgewise. It's nice to have someone in the house to take the focus off what I'm doing wrong."

Candace *tsked* at her. "You don't do anything wrong."

"Tell that to my Daed," Betsy said glumly. "I wouldn't worry about Micah, though. I'm sure he'll set the record straight soon. After all, his father didn't care who he married, just that he came home with a bride."

Candace froze. Came home? If she did wind up marrying Micah, she would have to move to Pennsylvania and leave her Daed all alone. She couldn't do that. He might not get over another loss. And she would be the sole source of income for a long time while his ribs healed. She couldn't leave. The realization hit her like cold water splashed in her face.

She couldn't marry Micah.

"Maybe you should marry him after all," Candace said softly.

"What?" Betsy asked, stopping halfway from the prep area to the oven.

Candace feared for the pie Betsy was holding and took it from her. "I know you're desperate for a home of your own. Micah can give you that as well as distance between your parents and even from Susan. Absence makes the heart grow fonder and all that." Feeling her heart splintering in her chest, she forced herself to continue. "I think you'd be happy with him." She slid the pie into the oven, welcoming the heat on her face to combat the cold inside her.

"A lot of people think that. My father. Amos's mother. But don't you like him?" Betsy trailed off as Candace bit her lip and turned away.

Candace knew she had to convince her friend that she had no interest in Micah. If Betsy even had a hint that she wanted more than anything to marry Micah, she would never consider him as a husband. Candace should have known better than to get her heart involved when so many people in Randolph considered Micah and Betsy stepping out to be a foregone conclusion.

"We're just friends." Candace swallowed hard and prayed that Gött would forgive her for not telling the complete truth. She and Micah *were* friends. "He's been so good to my father, and I'm so grateful to him. But I can't move to Pennsylvania. I need to marry someone local."

"Oh." Betsy turned back to the counter to start another batch of cookies. "Someone like Amos then." Candace couldn't read her friend's tone.

"I guess." Candace sighed. It wouldn't be a bad life. Just the same. Maybe Amos would even build her a studio so she could rent the space to her neighbor Krystal for her goat yoga when the weather was too chilly or rainy for outside exercise.

She didn't want to think about marriage right now. Not with

her father in the hospital and her sister-in-law about to give birth. If Micah needed a bride right away, it couldn't be her. No matter how happy that would make her.

But if he could wait a year, her father would be healed up and working again. Maybe he'd even consider marrying Judy. Then he wouldn't be alone.

"Do you know why Micah wants to get married right away?" she asked, hoping her voice conveyed that Betsy's answer made no difference to her.

"I think his father is eager for another farmer come harvesttime."

"Do you think he would wait?" She tried to push down the fluttering of hope in her breast.

"I think it's more his father that you'd have to convince. He seems very frustrated that Micah is determined to finish the construction contract. Even my father had to remind Ezekiel that it's important that the Mennonite company knows the Randolph Amish workers will finish a job that they've contracted for."

"I wonder if they'll ever hire my Daed again."

Betsy considered it. "I don't know. I don't see why they wouldn't. It's not as if he quit. He was injured on the job."

If he could work a job and have Judy to take care of him, Candace could consider going to Pennsylvania. She would just have to see if Micah and, more concerningly, Ezekiel, would be willing to wait another year.

One more year. She closed her eyes in a quick prayer. She wished she could skip to a year from now. Her father would be better. Esther's baby would be born. But if she did that, she would miss the little things, like seeing the Boppli grow and seeing her baby goats grow into adults. No, she didn't want to speed up time. She wanted Micah to wait a year to choose his bride, and she wanted that bride to be her.

14

Things were strained between Micah and his father, especially when he refused to come around to Ezekiel's way of thinking. He'd find a way to make his business work. If it meant he had follow the carpentry jobs around the Northeast until he could save enough money to buy some land, that was what he would do. Or he could take his father's acres and farm until his shop got on its feet. But that seemed unfair to his father. Micah wouldn't accept the land under false pretenses.

Valentine's Day came and went. Candace dropped off some cherry fry pies while he and his cousins were at work. He wanted to walk over and thank her, but his aunt said that Esther wasn't feeling up for visitors.

He comforted himself that he would see Candace tomorrow at the sugaring. Once the sap was boiled down and everyone was sampling it, he would use the distraction to try to explain what had happened and ask if she would still consider stepping out with him if he didn't have the promise of a farm and land.

At least his foreman, Lou, was pleased with his work and would keep him on the roster for the next project. He was sure that as long as he gave half of his paycheck to his Aenti, she would let him stay there until he got married. Then if he married Candace, he could stay at the Beacheys' house.

"It's only temporary," he told himself. "Just until I can build up my reputation and start selling cabinets." But would Lemuel allow him into his personal space?

Micah sighed. He was kidding himself. He didn't have anything to offer a bride, and he had no business asking Candace to step out with him until he did.

The next morning, he got up early to check on the taps and found the sap was flowing. They had hundreds of trees to gather sap from today. Amos and his brothers hitched the horse to the large trailer where an aluminum holding tank would store the sap they collected. Once the tank was full, they would take it down to the sugar shack, where Judy was already stoking the fire under the heavy-duty pans. They were returning with the first load of sap when Micah's father and the Millers arrived. The whole community would probably turn out today to help collect the large buckets of sap to boil down into maple syrup.

He was surprised to see that Betsy looked like she had been crying, and Micah hoped Amos didn't see her like that. He wondered what was going on. But before he could make his way over to her, his father approached him.

"We need to talk," his father said, taking him by the arm.

"I think we've said all that we are going to say on the topic of the farm. I'm not going to convince you and you're not going to—"

"You can have one acre. If you can fit a home and a workshop and a showroom on it, that's fine."

Micah cocked his head at his father. "What made you change your mind?"

"It doesn't matter. All you have to do is marry Betsy Miller next month before you come home and you can run your land as you see fit."

Closing his eyes, he chided himself. He knew he should have told him about Candace sooner. There would never be a good time, so he said, "I'm sorry, Daed. I can't marry Betsy Miller. I'm in love with Candace Beachey, and I'm going to ask her to marry me." Eventually. When he had something to offer her.

"Candace Beachey is your cousin Amos's girl."

"About as much as Betsy is mine. Amos is the man who wants to marry Betsy, not me."

His father stared at him, dumbfounded. "Could you have made this more complicated?"

"I'm sorry, Daed. I'm not trying to be difficult."

"You told me you were engaged to Betsy."

"Nee, I didn't. Both you and her father wanted that to be the outcome and just took it for granted that we would comply. Why is it so important that I marry her?"

"Because her father and I think it's the best match."

"Why?" Micah crossed his arms over his chest.

Ezekiel sighed and looked off into the distance. "I had wanted to tell you this once we were back home. Our congregation has decided that Bishop Isaac is too sick to continue his ministry and deserves to live out his remaining days without the pressures of being bishop. We had a service, and I was chosen to be the new bishop. Your name came up as a candidate for deacon, but you need to be married in order to accept the position if you're chosen. And when my time comes to step down, it is my hope you will become bishop after me."

Micah staggered on his feet. This didn't seem real. His father was accepting that he wanted to build cabinets instead of farm tobacco. And his community thought so highly of him that they had suggested he become a deacon, even at his young age and even though he wasn't yet married. "I don't know what to say."

"Of course the final decision is in Gött's hand, but I have faith that you could follow in my footsteps. If not as a farmer, then as a servant to our community. Betsy's father would be pleased to have his daughter marry into our family. I'm sure Candace is a nice girl, but her father has lost his way. I think he'll return to the fold eventually. But if he can't?

You're going to need a supportive wife. Betsy will be your rock. She'll be there to comfort you after you've comforted others. Candace will be very hurt and emotional if her father is shunned. You can be her friend, from a distance, but not her husband. Betsy is the right choice. She's seen firsthand the rigors of a bishop's life and sacrifice. She will never need or expect more than you have to give."

"But Amos—"

"Amos is a *gut* man and a hard worker. He's a skilled carpenter who will provide for his wife. You do not need to worry that Candace wouldn't be cared for. I know you young people think that love is how you should pick your wives, but love fades, and what's left is duty and companionship."

Micah thought about Lemuel Beachey grieving for his wife to the point of decimating his own health, both physically and spiritually. "Love doesn't fade. It just gets stronger."

"You are kind and empathetic, but you are not yet wise. In twenty years' time, you will remember this conversation and realize I am right."

"Why was Betsy crying then? She doesn't want to marry me any more than I want to marry her."

His father frowned and wouldn't meet his gaze. "Her father is very strict and has high expectations of her. Sometimes he can be brusque in his effort to instruct his daughter."

"Is he forcing her to marry me? Because I won't allow that."

"Nee, she readily agreed to the quick marriage and conceded that there wasn't any need to wait until after the harvest. She agreed it was better to have the ceremony before harvest begins and to already have your life established by the time it comes around. Betsy is ready to leave her retail job and devote her life to you. Can Candace say the same?"

He opened his mouth to say that of course she was, but he knew she wasn't. Not when her father was in the convalescent home.

"Why do I have to get married right away? What's wrong with next year? Or after the harvest?"

"They will be choosing the deacon in a few weeks. You need to be married to be considered. An opportunity like this won't come around again for decades. And as you know, we could use a younger deacon."

Micah knew that was true. He would answer the calling if he was chosen, even though it would be hard and take time away from work and family. If it was Gött's will, then so be it.

"Come on, Micah," Amos called. They were ready for another round of collections. He was in charge of driving the buggy this time.

"Think about it," his father said.

He would, but he wasn't sure he'd come up with any solutions.

The next day, when they got back from another trip around the maple forest, Micah saw that Candace had arrived. She looked ready to head out to the trees and help with the collection. He wanted to catch her before she disappeared into the group of friends and family where they wouldn't have a moment's peace.

"Hey," he said, coming up to her. "Can you help me with something?"

"Sure." She put down the gallon jugs of iced tea she had been carrying and followed him behind the wood stack.

"I wanted to apologize for not coming by and seeing how you were. I haven't even been able to visit Lemuel." Micah rubbed his hand over his face. "My Daed has been challenging, but I still should have made the time."

"That's all right. Daed hasn't been in the best of moods, so it's probably for the best. Things have been overwhelming for him, but I'm happy to say that his pain has lessened to a more bearable level."

"That's good to hear. When can he come home?" Micah shifted his weight uncomfortably. He had so much to say to her, and they had so little time before someone approached them and their conversation would no longer be private.

"As soon as the doctors let him. He'd be back on the job already if he had the range of movement for it. He's probably going to be in there until March at least."

"I bet he loves that."

She rolled her eyes. "He's been catching up on his reading and card playing. Your aunt visits him for several hours at a time, and I think it's a great help to him."

"She's happy to do it. It gives her something different than taking care of us boys. Speaking of which, I wanted to thank you for the fry pies. They were delicious. We all enjoyed them."

"You're welcome." She glanced over her shoulder. "I should check on how Esther is doing."

"Wait," he said, panicking. It was now or never. "I need to ask you something."

A wild look appeared in her eyes. "Nee you don't." She took a step back away from him.

It gave him pause. Maybe he had misread her feelings for him. "Do you have a dream?"

Candace blinked at him in confusion. "A what?"

"Like a plan on how you wanted your life to be?"

She raised an eyebrow quizzically at him. "Sure. Doesn't everyone?"

"What is it?" he asked.

"Why do you want to know?"

"It's important to me. If you tell me yours, I'll tell you mine."

She peeked over the woodpile. "We should really get back into the woods. There's a lot of sap to collect."

"The buggy is still being unloaded. We've got a few minutes."

Candace crossed her arms over her chest. "I already know your dream. You want to have a cabinet store and your own workshop."

"Do you have one like that?"

"Ja," she whispered. "But you'll laugh if I tell you."

"I won't laugh," he promised.

She shook her head and looked away. He felt a pang of disappointment. He really had wanted to know. He didn't want her to feel uncomfortable, though. "Did you know that my father has accepted the position of bishop in Autumnfield?"

"I'll have to offer him my congratulations."

"There's a deacon position opening up. To be considered for that position—"

"You need to be married."

"Right away," he said, taking her hand. "And I was wondering if you—"

"A goat yoga studio," she blurted out.

Micah stopped and stared at her. He couldn't have heard that correctly. "Goat yoga?"

Easing her hand out of his grip, she turned and walked briskly back toward the sugar shack.

"Wait, what does that mean?" he asked, running after her.

"It means my Englisch neighbor Krystal wants to rent my goats for her yoga classes and have tourists come in and do yoga with my goats jumping all over them."

"Do you know what yoga is?"

"I went to a few classes when I was on Rumspringa. Krystal is an instructor. It's stretching and breathing exercises. You hold poses to build up strength in your core." She circled her hand around her stomach.

Micah considered her words and then his own before answering. This was part of the reason he found her so engaging. She had wonderful ideas, and he would never get tired of talking to her about them. Betsy, on the other hand, wouldn't have these thoughts.

By the time Micah figured out how he wanted to tell Candace that yoga was probably going to be forbidden based on the *Ordnung*, they were following the sap wagon. He tried to keep his voice down. "I don't want to step on your dream, but from what I know of it, yoga isn't just exercising. It has its origins in other religions and spirituality that I don't think the bishop would approve of." And if Lemuel was renouncing his faith, Candace would be scrutinized harshly if she started this business.

"How do you know that?" She frowned up at him.

"Rumspringa," he said. "I took a college course on comparative religions."

"Most kids just go to the movies and drive fast cars during Rumspringa," Candace said tartly. "You got a job and went to school?"

"What can I say? I was a rebel. I always had a calling toward my faith and I wanted to understand other people's beliefs."

"And did you understand them?"

"I understood the general principles and tenants of them. Some were very outlandish and nothing I would believe could happen. And yet millions of people do believe. That's why I think faith is so fascinating." He steadied her as she stumbled in the mud. "It also made me glad to be baptized because I understood and believed in our Amish faith."

"Well, I wouldn't be doing the exercises. Krystal would run the classes, and maybe I could rent to her if I had my own studio, but she never told me it was a religion."

"It's not a religion. It's a spiritual exercise."

"I see. Well, it doesn't have to be yoga," she said. "It can just as easily be normal stretches and exercises. The point is to have the goats jump all over people."

Micah was wondering if she was making fun of him, but she seemed serious, almost wistful. "And you think people will pay for that?"

"I think I'll have a full house. Of course, once they're there, they will want to buy the goat-milk soap, lotions, and creams. Anything that gets them in the door will help. If they want to be trampled by happy goats, that's their business."

That made more sense.

"At first, Krystal wanted to have the yo—*exercise* classes on her front lawn," she went on, "but what if it had rained the night before or was raining during their session? Playing with goats is fun. Playing with them in the mud, not so much. So, then I wanted my Daed to build me an exercise studio. I could rent the space to Krystal so the classes could be indoors when the weather wasn't cooperating. That way she could do classes whenever and I wouldn't have to fret about the goats eating her roses."

"What did he say?" Micah checked a few buckets hanging from the tap on the next tree. He took two that were more than half full and handed them to her. He took two more that were almost filled to the brim and they walked together to the sap wagon. It was John's turn to drive, but Amos wasn't anywhere in sight. He didn't see Betsy either, which worried him.

"When I asked Daed about the studio, he laughed and said to ask my Mamm," Candace said.

"What did she say?" Micah tried to picture the solemn Lemuel laughing and couldn't. For the first time, he began to understand that Candace had lost both of her parents when her Mamm died, because a part of her Daed had died too.

"She said no. Actually, she first wanted to know if I was crazy. Then, she said no—after she had laughed at the idea."

"I'm sorry. No one should laugh at someone's dream."

Candace smiled. "It *is* a little silly, but it's mine."

He couldn't keep the words back any longer, not after talking about her dream, not with the way she smiled at the thought of it, not with how he would suddenly do anything to make it come true. "Candace, will you marry me?"

She dropped the buckets. Luckily, they landed in the snow and only a little of the sap splashed out. "But you need to get married as soon as possible, and I can't leave my family right now."

"You can always come back and visit them." He knew he was grasping at straws. How could he even ask this of her?

"All my other sisters and brothers have left Randolph. All Daed has left is me and Simon. And soon Simon is going to be very busy with another baby."

"I don't have to go back and be considered for a deacon," he said, reaching for her hand again.

"Ja, you do. You would be a wise, kind, and compassionate one. I couldn't rob a community of that." She squeezed his hand before letting it go and picking up her buckets again.

"Your father can move into our house," Micah said, aware that he was getting close to begging and not caring. He couldn't picture any other future than one where he was with her.

"Is it built? Because he's coming home soon to recover. He can't help build a house, and it would disappoint him if he couldn't."

Micah looked away, his hope suddenly gone. "Nee, the land isn't even prepared."

"Then I'm so sorry, but I can't marry you." Her eyes filled with tears.

"Please don't cry. I will find a way."

She shook her head. "Nee, it's okay. Betsy will make you a good wife."

"But I want you," he whispered.

Choking back a sob, she said, "Please don't say things like that. You'll make it harder than it has to be."

"I'm not sure that's possible."

Micah's mind whirled. There had to be a way to make this work, but the more he thought about it, the more hopeless it seemed.

It came down to a choice. He could stay in Randolph and marry Candace, where he would live in her father's house and share Lemuel's woodshop, if Lemuel allowed it. And while he still could be considered for deacon again, that would be several years in the future—if at all. Or he could marry Betsy and have everything he wanted—except Candace. The choice should have been simple, but it wasn't. He had to try one last time.

"If I marry you, I'll probably be disowned. Would you take me as I am? Penniless and without a home and having to depend on your father to employ me so I can provide for you?"

She gripped the handles of the bucket so tightly, her knuckles were white. For a moment, he thought he had changed her mind.

"I won't marry you, Micah. Please don't ask again." She straightened and walked away through the snow, and it was as if she were kicking aside the pieces of his broken heart instead of the powdery flakes.

That had been his best shot. He had tried. And failed.

15

Simon shook her awake. It was still dark out. It had taken Candace most of the night to fall asleep. Who cared if the cows waited another half hour to be milked?

"What? What?" she grumbled.

"I have to take Esther to the hospital. The baby is coming and the midwife says there could be a problem."

Candace jumped out of bed, suddenly wide awake. "I'll handle everything on this end. Go. Just go."

He nodded and bolted back down the stairs. Candace tried to get dressed in a hurry to tell Esther it would all be all right, but they were already in the buggy by the time she got downstairs. She looked at the clock. It was three thirty in the morning. Biting back a yawn, she wondered why Bopplin didn't want to be born around lunchtime instead of before the cows were up. She made breakfast for the boys, waking them up at four thirty to help her milk the cows.

Abraham was sulky and rubbed his eyes. "Cold. Hungry."

Me too.

"Stomp your feet to keep warm. Gabriel and I need to finish milking the cows and give them their breakfast and then we can eat. I made waffles, and we can use the new syrup we helped make yesterday."

He seemed slightly mollified by that. However, he started up again as they walked over to her Daed's farm to repeat the process.

"I want Mamm."

"She'll be home soon with your new baby brother or sister," Candace said. Her nerves jangled and her teeth chattered as well. There was so much to do, and all she wanted was to crawl back into bed and sleep. Luckily, she was working an afternoon shift, so she could at least get the house clean for the new baby.

She wished her Mamm could be here to see this. And to help. Once the chores were done and they were all fed to bursting with waffles and sausage patties, Candace put Gabriel in charge of keeping Abraham entertained until it was time for the older boy to walk to school. She used the time to scrub the floors and the bathrooms, making sure everything was extra clean.

After school, Gabriel would go over to his friend Levi's house until she got off work. After he had left for school, Candace carried Abraham from room to room with her and sang with him every hymn and silly song she could think of while she worked. When it was time for her to go to the Amish Market, she bundled him up and made a stop at the Eichers' farm.

Judy came to the door as she pulled up. "What brings you here?"

"Esther is having her baby," Candace said. "I have to work. Can I ask you a favor?"

"Of course."

"Would you watch Abraham and bring him to see my father this morning and tell him the *gut* news?"

"Sure, I was planning on going there anyway."

"I'm going to stop off at the hospital to check on them after work, and then I'll be back for him by suppertime."

"If they're not able to come home yet, come and have supper with us."

Pain broadsided Candace. She hadn't had a moment to think about her conversation with Micah. He had asked her to marry him. And she'd had no choice but to turn him down. The heartbreak was only lessened slightly that at least he would marry her best friend. Betsy deserved happiness, and she would make a good clergyman's wife.

"Amos would be thrilled," Judy added.

Candace doubted that. She didn't think she could sit at the same table with Micah, but she didn't want to hurt Judy's feelings. "Let's see what tonight brings."

Judy smiled and took Abraham. Her whole face brightened as she told him how much fun they were going to have today.

"Denki," Candace said, tears filling her eyes as she turned away. Judy would make a wonderful grandmother someday. Settling into the seat of the buggy, she wiped at the tears as they ran down her cheeks. She let Belle run, even though she knew it was dangerous. She would be late for work if she didn't hurry. But even after letting Belle run full out until she was exhausted, Candace still punched in ten minutes late.

Karen was waiting for her. "Again?"

"I know. I'm sorry. My sister-in-law went into the hospital early this morning to have her Boppli." Candace gave her a watery grin.

"Congratulations." Karen turned away. "I need you up front today," she called over her shoulder.

"I can't." Candace shook her head. "My nerves are shot. I'll make mistakes. Please let me stay in the back and bake. I need to calm myself. There's so much to do and baking relaxes me."

Karen stopped and frowned at her. "I don't have another cashier. Betsy is no good on the register and I'm short-staffed. I'm also going to need you to work full-time again."

Taking a deep shuddering breath, Candace placed her hand on her stomach. She shouldn't have had such a big breakfast. It was sitting in her stomach like a lead balloon. "My Daed is still in the convalescent home, and now that my sister has a new baby coming home, I'm actually going to need to take some time off."

Karen shook her head. "I can't give you any more time."

Candace felt someone come up behind her. "I can cover her hours," Betsy said.

A wave of gratitude washed over her. Candace knew how much Betsy hated to work full-time.

"If it was just in the bakery, that would be fine. But you and Mary don't like using the registers and I need a cashier."

Candace straightened her shoulders. "My family needs me."

"I know," Karen said. "And I'm not unsympathetic. But in these past three months your performance has slipped. You're constantly late. You make silly mistakes on the register, and I can't count on you to be here."

"I'm here now. I've been up since three and I've put in a full day's work already at home." Candace was mortified that her voice cracked.

"You've always been a good worker, but when I gave you the position it was with the understanding that you would work full-time. If you can't do that, I need to hire someone who will."

"But I can still work here part-time, right?" Candace asked.

"I'm sorry. I'm going to have to let you go."

Betsy gasped.

At first, Candace didn't get it. "Let me go where?"

Karen frowned. "I'm terminating your employment. We'll mail your last check to your house and box up whatever soaps and lotions don't sell at the end of the month."

"I-I see."

"If Candace doesn't work here anymore, then neither do I. I quit," Betsy said in a fury, tossing her apron at Karen's feet. "Come on." She grabbed Candace's arm and led her out back where their buggies were.

"Betsy," Candace started and had to stop. If she finished that statement, she would burst into tears and when the storm was over,

Candace wasn't sure if anything would be left of her or if she would be all washed away.

"You're in no condition to drive. Get in. I'll have my Mamm and Daed pick up your buggy."

"I don't know what to do," she whispered. Would she get in trouble with the bishop for being fired?

"I'm taking you home. You're going to get in bed and sleep. Then we're going to visit Esther and Simon in the hospital."

"But what about—"

"Nee. Nothing more than that. We're taking this one situation at a time."

Candace was numb. "How can I do this without a job?" Without any income, they would have to rely on Simon's paycheck. She wasn't sure he could support two families with that. Maybe she would have to sell her goats. She whimpered as the thought crushed her. She'd rather sell a cow, but they would use the cow's milk and butter more than a goat's.

Numbers flashed through her head. If she could get a good deal on flour, they could live on goat cheese sandwiches. She gave a slightly hysterical giggle. This couldn't be happening. "I'll go back. I'll work the register full-time. But then, who would help Esther and Daed?"

"Not another word. We'll figure it out after you get some rest."

Candace let Betsy drive her home while she tried to keep her mind as blank as possible. Without her paycheck or Daed's, and with another Boppli to feed, Candace wasn't sure how they were going to make ends meet until their gardens came into fruition.

Betsy helped her up the stairs to her bedroom. Candace kicked off her boots and slid between the covers.

Betsy tucked her in and said, "Things happen for a reason."

"Don't let me sleep all day," she forced out. "I don't want to give up."

"You're not giving up. You're regaining energy. I'll be back later with Gabriel, and we'll go to the hospital. Everything will be fine. I promise."

"Okay," Candace said. She had to believe that or she would come apart. She thought she would never quiet her mind enough to drift off, but sleep claimed her the second she closed her eyes.

Candace was already sitting up in bed when Betsy pushed open the door. "Gabriel is finishing his snack, and then we're going to all go up to the hospital to see Simon and Esther."

"Has there been any word?" she asked.

"Nee, not yet. But that's not uncommon."

"Gabriel and Abraham came so fast. What's taking so long this time?" Candace put her boots back on.

"Every baby is different."

"You didn't really quit the market, did you?" she asked as they went downstairs.

"I sure did. Karen can't fire my friend and expect me to stick around."

"She had a point," Candace said, glancing down in shame.

"You're a *gut* worker. Sure, you've had some issues lately. But you're more reliable than most of her employees. Karen should have been more understanding."

"What am I going to do?"

"We'll figure something out. Maybe one of our Englisch neighbors are looking for a housekeeper. We could clean houses together."

That didn't sound so bad. And then she realized that Betsy would be leaving Randolph soon. "When are you moving to Pennsylvania?"

Betsy paled. "I don't know."

"It has to be soon, right? Micah has to be back for the deacon vote."

"I don't want to talk about that," Betsy said. "He can't go anywhere until his job is done here, and that's not going to be for a couple of weeks."

At least Candace would have her friend for a little while longer. They piled into Betsy's buggy. Candace noticed that hers was back from the market. "I'll have to thank your parents for bringing Belle home for me."

"My Daed is mad at Karen. He had some strong words for her."

"He didn't have to do that for me."

"He would have done that for any of us. We stand by our own."

"What happened?" Gabriel asked between bites of his peanut butter-and-marshmallow cream sandwich.

Shame filled her as Candace opened her mouth to tell him that she had been fired from the Amish Market, but Betsy beat her to it.

"Aenti Candace and I are no longer working at the Amish Market. They weren't treating us well. So, we're going to find another job. Maybe housekeeping."

"You should open a bakery together."

Candace smiled at him. The job change didn't faze him. He trusted that they would handle it. She wished she had that confidence.

"That's not a bad idea. I'd rather open one with you than with my sister," Betsy said, handing her a sandwich and a thermos of coffee. "You skipped lunch. This should tide you over until supper."

Supper with the Eichers and Micah. She wasn't looking forward to telling them—him—about losing her job. But they would find out sooner or later, and it was better if it came from her.

If Candace were honest with herself, she wasn't upset that she wouldn't be working at the market. She would miss the big ovens and the employee discount, but she wouldn't miss punching buttons on the cash register or dealing with irate customers. She could spend her time keeping up with housework and cooking. She could build up her stock of goat-milk soap and lotions and take them around to other stores to see if they would sell them on consignment. And there was still her Mamm's cookbook to finish.

They would get by. Her Mamm had taught her how to stretch meals, and if Simon went back to work right away, they would be fine until his contract was up. And even then, there was still the chance he would get another carpentry job. The Mennonite company seemed to like his work. And it would be even better when Daed could go back to work.

By the time they made it to the hospital, Candace was feeling like her old self again. The nap and sandwich had greatly improved her outlook. She was looking forward to seeing how Esther was doing. However, when they got to the hospital, Esther was still in labor, and they couldn't get any information from the grim-faced nurses. They waited around for a few hours, but Gabriel was getting nervous and restless. No doubt he was picking up on her anxiety. She must be calm.

Candace pulled Betsy aside. "Do you think you can take Gabriel home and pick up Abraham from Judy's?"

"Sure, but what are you going to do?"

"I'll stay here until I hear something. However long it takes." Candace bit her fingernails until she realized what she was doing.

"All right, don't worry about anything. I'll ask Amos and Micah to take care of the animals until you get back."

"Denki, I really appreciate it."

Betsy put her hand on her arm. "It's going to be all right."

"You keep saying that."

"It's because it's true. Take as much time as you need. Send word if you can."

"I will." She gave Betsy a quick hug. Candace would miss her friendship when she married and left for Pennsylvania, to say nothing of how she would miss her friend's husband-to-be—his generosity, his strength, and his way of steadying her whether her slip was literal or figurative.

The realization crashed over her that all she wanted right now was for Micah to be here with her.

16

Micah was worried about the Beacheys. Esther's labor had gone on longer than it should have and infection had set in. Both the baby girl and her mother were fighting fevers, and the whole community was worried. Everyone had pitched in to keep both farms going while Candace and Simon took shifts at the hospital, hoping for a change.

The past week had been grueling for everyone. The Mennonite company was pressuring them to finish the job as soon as possible. They wanted to come in under budget and with two men out, it made the job more stressful for everyone. Then back home, his father suggested that he quit to go home early with him, and Betsy's father was asking her if she wanted to get married in Autumnfield or here in Randolph. So far, she'd managed to not answer that question.

He and his cousins were pitching in to help at the Beacheys' farms at night because there wasn't time in the mornings. Micah didn't think Simon had been back to the farm for anything longer than a quick sleep between visiting hours, and that's only when they kicked him out of the hospital. When Candace wasn't at the hospital, she was watching her nephews and trying to keep things as normal as possible for them. But when Gabriel was at school, she often dropped Abraham off with Aenti Judy and went up to the hospital to try and give her brother a break.

On Saturday, Micah went to the convalescent home to visit Lemuel. Judy had mentioned that she had been his only visitor all week, and he was desperate for news about his family.

"Has there been any word?" Lemuel asked when he came in.

He was sitting up in bed, still looking gaunt and weak, but there was a determination in him that Micah didn't remember seeing before. Aenti Judy was there, keeping him company. She looked up from her knitting and smiled at him.

"There's been no change," Micah said quietly.

"What are you doing?" Judy gasped, scandalized as Lemuel swung his legs off the bed.

"I am going to see my family."

Judy hurried out of the room. "I'm getting the doctor."

Micah closed the door behind her. "Are you sure you're up for this?" he asked.

"My family needs me."

Micah found the clothes Lemuel had worn to the hospital, and Lemuel did a good job of dressing himself. It was slow going, and he was obviously stiff and in pain. He managed everything but tying his shoes and getting his suspenders over his shoulders. But with Micah's help, he was soon ready.

A nurse came in just as they were finishing. "Where do you think you're going?"

"My daughter-in-law just had a baby, and I'm going to see them."

"I-I'll have to check with the doctor," she stammered.

"You do that," Lemuel said, and when she left, he turned to Micah. "Let's go. While they're trying to find a doctor, we can just walk on out of here as if we don't have a care in the world."

"I'm pretty sure that's against the rules," Micah said, both amused and concerned.

"They can scold me when I return," he replied, putting on his hat and setting the brim low on his forehead.

"Do you want a wheelchair?"

"I can walk."

"What if they stop us?"

"They won't. We Amish all look alike to them. But we have to leave before Judy gets back."

"Too late," Judy said from the doorway. "The doctor will be here any second."

"I'm leaving." Lemuel took a step outside the door. "I'm tired of these snippets of information that don't actually tell me anything. I am going to go to my children. They need their father."

Micah waited to see if Judy was going to stop him, but she just sighed and looked around for help. She found none. This wasn't a hospital and there wasn't a central nurse station, so they were able to walk down the halls without being questioned or stopped. The doctors and nurses were likely busy with other patients. They took their time, and with Judy hovering and circling, they left the building. Micah hadn't expected to be part of a "jail break." He had just wanted to talk to Lemuel.

"I'm not going to drive you," Judy said, folding her arms across her chest. "This is madness. You're going to relapse or hurt yourself."

"Micah, would you take me to see my family?"

He sounded so solemn and sad, Micah couldn't refuse him. And he knew Candace would never forgive him if she found out her father had finally begun to show signs of life and Micah had stopped him. With an apologetic look at his aunt, he said, "Ja, my buggy is over here."

"You are going to get in trouble." Judy wagged her finger at them.

"I'll make sure to bring him back after," Micah said. "Why don't you go home and check on Abraham and Gabriel? Daed was having them work in the garden. I'm sure they could use some milk and cookies."

"Don't try to distract me," Judy said. "Betsy and her mother have that well in hand. And don't think for one second that I'm not going to tell the bishop about this. This is your last chance, Lemuel Beachey. Come to your senses and go back inside."

"Thank you for your visit today, Judy," Lemuel said when they reached Micah's buggy.

"How are we supposed to get him in the buggy?" Judy asked in exasperation.

"It'll take me a bit, but I can do it." Grunting, Lemuel lifted himself up and into the buggy. Micah saw the thin sheen of sweat on his brow and the pain in his eyes.

"You're an old fool," Judy scolded.

"I hurt worse doing that infernal physical therapy." His voice had only a trace of breathlessness in it.

Micah hauled himself up into the driver's seat. With a nod to his aunt, he pulled away from the convalescent home. It did feel a little like he was aiding and abetting a fugitive, but he figured if they really wanted Lemuel back, they could catch him pretty easily. Micah's horse didn't move anywhere near as fast as their vehicles. He checked over his shoulder, but no one was following them.

Lemuel seemed to be sitting up straighter. Micah suspected that the crisp, fresh air was doing him a world of good. "How are Simon and Candace?" he asked.

"Simon is a wreck," Micah said. "Candace is barely holding everything together." He hadn't seen them all week, but his aunt had told him that.

Lemuel nodded.

Micah wondered what was going through his mind right now, and if he was strong enough both physically and mentally to handle seeing his children like this.

"Who did you say was watching Abraham and Gabriel?"

"Betsy and her family," Micah said. His Daed was keeping the boys' spirits up as well, by having them help him plant spinach and lettuce at the Beachey farms. Micah thought the ground might still be too cold for that, but he wasn't the expert that his father was. Besides, it was keeping the boys busy and keeping their minds off their mother and baby sister.

"How's the children's center going?"

"We're almost done." Micah took a deep breath. He had come to visit him to ask him an important question. He might as well get it over with.

"And you'll be heading back to Autumnfield?"

"Eventually." He was in no hurry to leave Candace. "I was hoping to get your permission to build something on your land before I go."

Lemuel tried to turn toward him, but his range of movement didn't quite allow for it. "What?"

"I want to build Candace her goat studio."

"Why on earth would you want to do that?" Lemuel asked in amazement.

Micah paused, realizing that Lemuel might not know that Candace had lost her job. Well, it was no use stopping now. "Because she was fired from her job at the Amish Market and she's feeling kind of low. My cousins and I could build her a studio so she can start up her own business."

"Where are you going to get the money for the supplies?"

"Lou said he could get me a good deal on lumber in exchange for me doing some cabinetwork."

Lemuel cocked his head at him. "That's smart negotiating. Do you feel you're ready to do that?"

"I could use some help," Micah admitted with a small smile.

"I might have some free time." A sly smile crept over Lemuel's face. "Why don't you build this studio on your own land?"

Micah forced out a humorless laugh. "I asked your daughter to marry me and she turned me down."

"She what?" Lemuel yelled, and then rubbed his chest as a twinge of pain flashed across his face. "Why on earth would she do a crazy thing like that?"

"She doesn't want to marry me," Micah said, trying and failing to keep his tone light. "I don't know why."

"Nonsense. I'll talk some sense into her." Lemuel rubbed his jaw in thought.

"She wants me to marry Betsy Miller."

Lemuel snorted. "She does not. I'm not sure what's going on, but from what I've seen, Candace really likes you."

"I really like her too. I think she's wonderful."

"She can be a handful," Lemuel said. "Just like her mother. Sarah kept me on my toes, and Candace would do the same to you. It would be *gut* for you, though."

"My father and Bishop Mark also want me to marry Betsy."

"And what do you want? What does Betsy want?"

"Betsy and I aren't too keen on the idea, but I need a wife soon because I'm being considered to become a deacon in my church."

"That's a great responsibility for one as young as you are. What would you tell one of your flock if they came to you with the same problem?" Lemuel asked.

"I'd tell them to follow their heart. But that's just the thing—my heart is split."

Lemuel shook his head. "Nee, it's not. You know where your heart is. You're willing to settle. It would be a great injustice to you, Betsy, Candace, and, I believe, young Amos Eicher if you did."

"If I don't marry Betsy, my father won't give me any land to build on. Candace deserves a house of her own."

Lemuel nodded slowly. "I see. Well, in that case, you have my permission to build a studio on my property. Candace can rent it out to someone else once Englischers get tired of little hooves jumping on them."

"Denki."

"And you also have my permission and approval to marry my daughter. Not that you need it. And not that you need your parents' approval either."

"I'd need the bishop's approval," Micah pointed out.

"You let me handle him."

"Both of them?" he asked hopefully. "My Daed was recently chosen to be our community's next bishop."

Lemuel chuckled. "You're on your own with your father."

"I was afraid you were going to say that."

The approval he really needed was Candace's, and she had told him not to ask her again. Micah was still not sure how this would all work out, but at the very least, Candace would have a studio. He would get his cousins to work on it this week, and if they could raise a barn in a few days, he was sure they could get a studio up and finished in a few weeks. Especially now that it was his last few weeks on the carpentry job.

After he hitched up the buggy at the hospital, he asked Lemuel to wait while he got a wheelchair. When Lemuel was going to balk, Micah told him it was a long way to get to where Esther was and he would need his strength. Lemuel grudgingly agreed. Once he was settled into the chair, Lemuel seemed content to be whisked around the hospital.

They found the right elevator after a few wrong turns and were soon on their way to the neonatal unit. They weren't allowed in, but Micah was able to wheel Lemuel by and catch Candace's eye through the window. She was sitting next to the baby, reading aloud from a prayer book. When she looked up and saw them, she did a double take. She closed the book and hurried outside the room.

"Daed, what are you doing here?"

"I've come to see my granddaughter. Can she have visitors?"

"Ja, up to three including me or Simon. Or Esther, of course."

"How is Esther?" Micah asked as she held the door open for him to wheel Lemuel through.

"Still very sick. Simon only leaves her side to come here."

"Everything is all right at home. I don't want you to worry," Micah said.

Candace shook her head. "Truthfully, it's the last thing on my mind right now." She followed them in.

"What's her name?" Lemuel asked.

Catching her breath, Candace hesitated. But when her father peered at her, she murmured, "Sarah. They named her after Mamm."

Tears filled Lemuel's eyes, and he studied the baby. "She's so tiny."

"She's running a fever, but she has the best care."

There was a knock on the door. "Oh, Daed, Simon is here."

"I'll wait outside," Micah said.

"I'll go with you. I want to say hello to Esther if she's awake."

When they stepped outside, Micah was concerned by how haggard and exhausted Simon looked. "Denki for bringing my father here. I didn't think he'd be well enough to come or I would have done it. I've been meaning to go and see him." Simon ran his hand through his hair. "I just haven't had time."

"No one expects you to be anywhere but here," Micah said.

Lemuel got up from his chair, his gaze on his son through the window.

"Nee, Daed, don't get up," Simon protested, going through the door. "It's *gut* to see you. How are you feeling?"

Micah closed the door to give them some privacy. "I've been worried about you," he told Candace.

"Me?" She wiped her eyes. "I'm not the one lying in a hospital bed."

"But you are the one holding everything together."

"I try, but most days I don't feel like I'm succeeding." She walked down the hall and he followed.

"You're too hard on yourself."

"How have you been?" she asked abruptly.

"I'm keeping busy. I've got a new project to work on before I go home."

"When will that be?" she asked, her hand over her heart.

He looked into her eyes and knew that she didn't want him to go any more than he did. "When I'm done with my project," he said.

"I'll write to you . . . and Betsy," she added quickly, looking down.

Micah wanted to tell her that he didn't want to marry Betsy, but he didn't want to add to her burden.

She opened the door to Esther's room and peeked in, then closed it. "She's asleep. I don't want to disturb her. Her fever is still very high and she's sometimes delusional."

"We will all pray for her and baby Sarah," he said, his mind flitting back to his sister, another baby Sarah.

"Oh, I left my prayer book with the baby. I should go and get it so I can say some prayers by Esther too."

As they walked back to the neonatal section, she asked, "What project are you working on?"

"It's a surprise," he said.

"For Betsy?"

"It's a secret." He smiled at her.

"Micah," she said, her voice ending on a sob. "I will miss you so much when you go." She hid her face. "And Betsy, of course."

He longed to put his arms around her and tell her that everything would be all right, but it would be inappropriate. "I will always be there for you," he said instead.

She put her hand over her face. "The things you say." Her voice shook. "Oh, Micah. I wish things were different."

"If they were, would you marry me?"

She looked up into his eyes, tears sparkling in her lashes. "Of course I would."

Joy hit him like a blast of sunlight and he knew what he would do. Candace took a shuddering breath and lifted a trembling hand to cup his cheek. All too soon, she removed her hand and approached the room. She stopped dead in her tracks, her body so still that Micah grew worried.

"Candace?" He put a hand on her shoulder.

"Look." She pointed.

Simon was slumped in a chair, sound asleep.

"He probably needed it. Why don't we go down to the cafeteria with Lemuel and have something to eat?"

Clutching his arm, she said, "Nee, look."

Micah peered through the window again and gasped. Lemuel had picked up Candace's prayer book and was reading it to the baby. Micah heard a sob beside him and suddenly didn't care about propriety anymore. He gathered Candace into his arms and hugged her tightly as she cried into his shirt.

17

Her father was coming home today. Whether that little stunt he pulled at the convalescent home was the last straw for them or whether he was truly healthy enough to come home, Candace wasn't sure. What she did know was that Lemuel Beachey wanted to come home, and she was ready for him to come back too. She moved his bedroom to the one on the ground floor so he wouldn't exacerbate his condition going up and down the stairs. She had no doubt that he would strain something helping Micah and his cousins build the new workshop out back.

It was good to be back in her own home, concentrating on cooking and cleaning again. And while she wasn't quite sure how they were going stretch their finances until their gardens came in, Candace had faith that Gött would provide.

He had certainly answered all their prayers about Esther and baby Sarah. Their fevers were down and their infections almost gone. They would be coming home, too, by the end of the week, just in time for church, which was at Betsy's house. Micah and Betsy would probably formally announce their engagement then. She wondered if she could manage to look happy for them.

She would be happy for them.

Eventually.

Looking out the window, she watched Micah and his cousins carry wood and hammer beams into place as she washed dishes. It was going to be a big structure with plenty of natural sunlight. Micah said her father had drawn up the plans himself. Hopefully, he would take it easy this afternoon when he came home, but Candace had a feeling he'd be out there giving his two cents, if not trying to saw wood or hammer planks. She could watch Micah all day, but that wouldn't get the kitchen in order or the bread started for tonight's meal. She didn't miss the Amish Market one bit, but she knew that would change on payday. Still, she had until the end of the month for her soaps and lotions to sell, and that would be a welcome addition, in any amount.

Once the kitchen was clean and the rolls were in the oven, she decided to spend some more time on her Mamm's recipes. Candace had decided that in addition to a daily menu, she would also include special-occasion menus. Her Mamm's happy day cake recipe would go under birthday parties and other celebrations. Candace had planned to make one for Esther and Sarah's homecoming, and maybe she would make one for her Daed too. After all, Micah and the Eichers were going to have supper with them.

She had made the cake so many times that she didn't even need the recipe. As she measured out the flour and the sugar, she could almost hear her Mamm's voice gently instructing her as she had done when Candace was Gabriel's age. She whipped up the buttercream frosting after setting the cake batter on the counter to wait its turn in the oven. She had to admit she missed one thing about the market. That big oven could hold a whole week's worth of rolls and desserts.

The sound of a buggy approaching made her frown. Simon had said he was going to pick up Gabriel after school and take him with him to help Daed gather his things from the convalescent home. Abraham was spending the day playing with their neighbor's little boy, who was the same age as he was. Betsy and her family were probably knee-deep in church cleaning and cooking. So who was coming to visit her?

She came to the door and froze. It was Micah's father.

Candace wasn't sure why that made her nervous. Maybe because he was about to become a bishop in Autumnfield.

"Hello, Ezekiel," she said. "Micah and the boys are out back."

"I've actually come to see you, Candace."

That couldn't be good, could it?

"Oh, um, please come in. I'll put some coffee on. Or would you prefer tea?"

"Tea would be fine."

"Make yourself comfortable in the living room. I'll be right in."

Bustling around the kitchen, she peered out the window again, willing Micah to come rescue her so she didn't have to face his father all alone. But it was apparent that wasn't going to happen, so when the tea was ready, Candace carried it to the living room on a serving tray, stocked with milk, sugar, and the leftover cookies from lunch. It was a good thing she was used to baking for an entire store of people.

She poured them each a cup of tea and perched on the edge of the comfortable chair facing the couch, where he sat. Isn't this what she'd daydreamed about when she was working at the market—a chance to share tea and conversation with someone?

He sipped his tea and watched her, saying nothing.

After a few minutes, Candace could bear the awful silence no longer. "What can I do for you?"

"I came to thank you."

She blinked at him. "You're welcome, I'm sure, but what did I do?"

"I'm sure Micah has told you that I had high hopes for him to be a farmer."

"That's not his calling," she said with what she hoped was a winning smile.

"Nee," Ezekiel said reluctantly. "His true calling is helping people."

"You only have to look outside to see that," she said. "Micah is a fine man. You've done a great job in raising him to be kind and compassionate. I don't know how I would have gotten through the grief over my Mamm's passing and my family's troubles if it weren't for your son."

"You helped me understand Micah better. I can see you care for him deeply."

"I love him," she said simply.

His expression was troubled. "I think he loves you too."

Tears sprang into the corner of her eyes. "Did you know he asked me to marry him?"

Shock flickered across his face. "When was this?"

"At the sugaring. I had to tell him no," she said, staring at her fingers wrapped around her cup.

"I don't understand. You just told me you love him."

"Cabinetmaking is how he wants to support his family, but helping people is the core of who he is. He told me that he is being considered for a deacon's position."

"His name was one of the first to come up. The only hesitation was that he is not married. I knew that it was only a matter of time before our beloved Bishop Isaac would be stepping down, so I tried to make finding a wife as easy for him as possible."

"Betsy will make him a good wife," she said with a small smile.

"Candace, you haven't answered my question. Why didn't you accept his offer of marriage?" Ezekiel put his teacup on the saucer and stared at her as if to draw the answer out.

"I can't leave my father right now. And Micah can't miss this opportunity. I'm sure it would have come around again for him in however many years, but any community would be better with Micah as a deacon for as long as they could have him."

Ezekiel straightened up in his seat. "You're a remarkable young woman, Candace. I wasn't expecting you to be sensible. I know you both think you're in love, but take it from me—love fades."

She shook her head. "With all due respect, sir, you are wrong. My parents had a love that didn't fade."

"And look how that ended for your Daed. When he lost his wife, it broke him. I wouldn't want that for you or my son."

Anger flashed through her. Her father was going through troubles, but what person didn't? She wouldn't have traded a minute of her childhood to save her the pain of her Mamm passing. And she knew her father felt the same way about his marriage. He didn't regret one moment of it, and now that he was coming out on the other side of his grief, perhaps he would move on eventually and get remarried. And she would be happy for him.

But it was too soon to expect that he would do so now. She didn't resent her father for being the reason she couldn't marry Micah. That was how she had been raised, and she was happy to do her duty. Just as Micah had been raised to help people and not turn his back on someone in need, Candace wouldn't abandon her family when they needed her.

"So why did you come here?"

"Betsy and Micah are going to make their engagement announcement after church next Sunday. I wanted to prepare you for that."

Pain made her mute, so she only nodded. Candace didn't know why the news hurt so much when she had been expecting it, but she could barely breathe.

He got up, and she walked him to the door. Candace mustered a pleasant expression for him, but she couldn't manage a smile.

"At least now I know why he's building that studio for you," he said.

"Studio?" she blurted, finding her voice in spite of the shock that pulsed through her. "Nee, it's a new workshop for my father. He designed it, and since his ribs have not fully recovered yet, Micah is helping him build it. As a thank-you for showing him some woodworking techniques."

Ezekiel shook his head. "That's not what he told me. I couldn't figure out why he wanted to build it for you, but I understand now. You have a dream of running your own business."

She blinked at him. "I do." She wasn't going to get into the goat part of it right now.

"He wanted to give you your dream." Ezekiel smiled at her. "I wish you all the best. If things were different, I would have loved to have you as a daughter-in-law."

"Denki," she whispered, still reeling from his words. She barely noticed when he got into his buggy and left. Wandering over to the back door, she stared at the structure. That was going to be her shop. She could sell her baked goods, soaps, and lotions there if she wanted. Or she could have the goats in for the exercise programs.

Clinging to the doorframe for support, she knew that whatever happened—if her goat yoga was a bust or if she never sold a single pie—she would always walk into that studio and think of Micah.

Esther's presence was missed at Lemuel's welcome-home meal, but she and the baby were still going to be in observation for a few days.

Candace was the only female at a table full of men. But it made her heart happy to see all of them eat so heartily. Her father had his color back. Simon looked a little more at peace. Micah and his cousins were tired from a full day's work, but everyone was enjoying her chili. She'd made a huge batch because it was economical and everybody loved it, especially paired with thick chunks of homemade corn bread slathered in fresh butter. No one would leave her table hungry, and there were even leftovers for supper tomorrow. Watching Simon tuck into the chili, she made a mental note to put together some casseroles and breakfast quiches for her brother and Esther so they would have easy meals once the baby and Esther were allowed to come home.

Candace was worried about the hospital bill. Unlike her father's injury, they didn't have insurance for this, and they would have to write a check for the services very soon. They would have to go on a payment plan and petition the bishop to use the community funds to help. They would make do, but she was a little disheartened by the steep expense.

She was surprised when Micah helped her carry the dishes into the kitchen. "You don't have to do that," she protested. "You've done so much already. Go sit in the living room and relax. I'll bring out dessert in a few minutes."

"I wanted to spend some time with you."

Candace was desperate for time with him as well. She wasn't sure how she was going to manage when he was her best friend's husband. But then again, they would move to Pennsylvania and she probably would only visit them once a year, if that. "Your father came to visit today."

"Here?"

"Ja. He and I had a chat, and then he left."

"He could have stayed and nailed a few boards," Micah grumbled.

"He told me you were going to announce your engagement to Betsy in church."

Micah sighed. "I'm not sure why he thinks that, considering I haven't asked her yet. I've still got two more weeks at the construction job and your Daed's workshop isn't finished yet."

Candace didn't tell him that his father had also spilled the beans about Daed's new workshop actually being her goat studio. She wouldn't ruin his surprise for the world.

"I guess he doesn't want you waiting until the last minute," she said lightly.

"That's what I came in here to talk to you about. I've made a decision," Micah said. "I'm not going to marry Betsy."

Candace gasped. "You can't. You have to get married right away."

"Only if I'm going to be considered for the open deacon position in Autumnfield. I no longer believe that is the right path for me."

"Of course it is," she said. "You'll have to wait several years, maybe more, for another chance."

"So I'll wait. I'd rather do that than marry the wrong person."

Candace's heart pounded. She didn't dare think beyond this moment or try to guess what Micah's intentions were, just in case she was wrong. She would be crushed. "Your father, though. He's going to be so angry."

Micah nodded. "I'll probably be staying at Aenti Judy's house on a more permanent basis. But you'll get to see me more often, and maybe when things settle down a bit, you'll reconsider my offer of marriage. It still stands. It will always stand."

Candace started to cry. This was what she wanted after all, but she felt so guilty.

"Please don't cry. This is a *gut* thing. And more importantly, it is the right thing."

She shook her head. "It's not. You'll lose everything."

"Nothing that can't be replaced. I gain my heart's desire. That is, if you'll have me."

"Micah, I can't marry you until my father is more settled. He's suffered so much since my Mamm died. I don't know how long it will be until he'll be ready to lose me too. Maybe in a few years, he'll consider remarrying. I don't want you to wait that long."

Micah took the bowl from her hands and dunked it into the soapy water. "Some things are worth waiting for."

She used the dish towel to dry her face and when she looked up, she saw her father in the doorway. How much had he heard? "Dessert will be right up," she said, forcing a bright, happy tone into her voice.

Lemuel responded with his usual grunt and walked back out of the kitchen.

"So," Micah said, "if my father wants me to make an announcement of whom I'm going to marry, I'm not going to name Betsy Miller. If it's all right with you, I'm going to say your name."

Her knees trembled and she steadied herself on the counter. "Micah . . ." She wanted to talk him out of this for his sake, but a selfish part of her held her tongue.

"Our engagement can be as long as you want. Since I won't be going back to Autumnfield, we can get married whenever. I could help your Daed with the woodworking and chores." He brushed his thumb over her cheek. "So you see, I'm not giving up anything important. And I'm gaining the world."

"But you're giving up your home and your father's approval. Won't you come to resent me?"

"Will you resent me that I came into this marriage with nothing to offer you?"

"Nothing?" A smile broke over her face. "I only need you."

"Then it's settled. I'll talk to my Daed and the bishop tonight. I'm going to need their approval to marry."

"What if they refuse?" Candace asked. It wasn't fair to come this far only to be shut down.

"They can't force me to marry Betsy Miller if I don't want to," he said.

There was a choking sound in the doorway, and they both whirled to see Amos standing there. "I-I was just wondering whether the coffee was ready."

She closed her eyes and almost groaned. "Just a few more minutes," she said, trying for a pleasant tone.

Amos nodded and disappeared again.

"You start the coffee and I'll finish the dishes," Micah said, nudging her away from the sink.

"We should take a little more time," Candace said drily. "Simon hasn't come in yet."

"They just all love your cake and coffee."

Candace put the percolator on. "Well, they're just going to have to wait a bit longer."

"The cake looks nice," he said, his calm tone soothing her.

While she waited for the coffee, she piped *Welcome Home, Daed* on it in white icing because she used chocolate to frost it.

"I'm sorry that this will cause problems in your family," Candace said. "Are you sure this is what you want?" She had to give him one last chance to come to his senses.

He finished drying the last plate and set it on the counter, then took her hands and gazed into her eyes. She was overwhelmed by the love, the steadiness, and the peace she saw there. "I've never been more sure of anything. I wish my Daed would give me land for my workshop without using poor Betsy as a bribe, but Betsy and I wouldn't be happy together. This is the right thing to do."

"I hope so."

Simon walked in the kitchen and Candace yanked her hands away. "The coffee isn't ready yet," she snapped at him.

He held a note in his hand. "There's a problem."

"Esther and the baby?" Candace put a hand over her heart. She thought they were out of the woods.

"Not exactly," he said.

"If you want, I can give you two some privacy," Micah said.

"Nee, this concerns you too. And I'm not sure how I'm going to say this, so I'm going to let the bishop speak for himself." He cleared his throat and read from the letter he was holding. "'Dear Simon, I appreciate you bringing the hospital bills over to me so quickly. I'm afraid I won't have time to look them over until after Micah announces his engagement to my Betsy next week.'"

Candace didn't care if Simon was in the room or not. She put her hand on Micah's arm. His jaw was clenched.

"'I think it's for the best that Betsy goes to Pennsylvania as soon as possible to be married. Her friendship with Candace has cost her a lucrative job—'"

"One she disliked and only went to because her father made her go," Candace broke in.

Simon continued reading. "'I would hate for it to cost her a husband as well. I hope you will do everything in your power to make sure that Candace realizes that Amos is a better match for her.'"

"He can't do that, can he? Not pay Esther's medical bills?" Candace asked.

Micah closed his eyes and took in a deep breath through his nose. "He probably can."

"But if you do marry Betsy, the bishop will authorize the community funds for the medical bills," Simon said. His face was ashen. "That's blackmail."

She didn't understand any of this. This wasn't how Amish communities were supposed to work.

Micah shook his head. "Daed thinks I'm still a child who needs instruction. I guarantee you this is their way of trying to control me. I'm so sorry your family has gotten involved in this. How much is the hospital bill, if you don't mind me asking?"

"Over fifty thousand dollars," Simon said.

Candace gasped, her hand over her mouth. They didn't have that. They didn't have anywhere close to that. They were even running low on grocery money, since Simon had been off work for the last week tending to Esther.

"We were prepared for the cost of a normal birth, but the complications and the long stay were not anticipated," Simon said.

"We can get on a payment plan," she said, desperately. She'd do whatever it took, contribute everything she made from rent on the studio and the items she sold. She'd get another job. She—

"I'm going to walk home. Please excuse me."

Candace moved to follow him, but Simon blocked her from going. "It isn't right for you to chase after him."

"I'm not chasing. I just want to talk to him."

"You can talk with him tomorrow," Simon said. "Come, serve the coffee and I'll get the cake."

She obeyed her brother, even though every nerve in her body was demanding that she do the opposite. She had a terrible fear that tomorrow would be too late.

18

Micah had never been so reluctant to go to church in his life. After work one day, he had spoken to Bishop Mark, and the bishop confirmed that if Micah married Candace, he wouldn't approve the community funds for Esther and Simon Beachey.

Talking with his father didn't give him any better results. His Daed was holding firm too. If Micah married Candace instead of Betsy, he wouldn't have any land or money coming to him to start his family.

Micah didn't dare talk to Lemuel. He didn't want to put pressure on his friend when his newfound peace was so fragile. Micah had come to terms that he would be penniless if he married Candace, but now he would be costing her family the money they needed to pay off their medical bills. It could take decades to pay them in full. He didn't want that hanging over their heads.

And that's what he told Candace. She took the news better than he had. She said she would pray to be happy for them, and she was glad that at least he had a chance of becoming a deacon if he married Betsy right away.

"The new workshop—it's not for your Daed," Micah confessed. "I built it for you and your goats."

She burst out crying and laughing then, and the only thing he could think to do was to hold her close. It would be the last time.

"I'm so sorry I've caused you so much heartache," he whispered.

"Never be sorry. I'm not. I never will be." She stepped away. "Promise me something."

"Anything."

"Don't be like our bishop. Don't force young lovers apart, even if you think you're right. Even if you think you know better."

"I promise," he said with his hand over his heart.

"I'll hold you to that, Micah Zehr." She stood on tiptoe and kissed him swiftly on the cheek, then hurried inside.

He would carry that scandalous kiss in his heart forever.

The church felt stifling, although the late March temperature was barely above fifty degrees. He'd spent only three months in Randolph, yet it felt like he had lived here all his life. At first he had longed for home, with the bustle of the crowds of tourists and the wide-open spaces of the farms around their property. But now, he knew he was going to miss the closeness of this community, in spite of everything that had happened here. He desperately didn't want to marry Betsy Miller, and if he could have skipped church today, he would have. It wasn't that Betsy was a bad choice for a wife. It was just that she wasn't his choice.

His true choice was sitting across the room with Esther and her new Boppli. *Sarah*, he thought with a smile, thinking of his baby sister. Micah nodded to Lemuel and Simon as they came in. They sat down a few chairs away on his left with Gabriel and Abraham between them. He was glad that Lemuel had come to church again. It was unfortunate he'd had to find his faith by praying over his granddaughter and his daughter-in-law, but it had healed him. Micah sensed a core of strength in him that he hadn't had access to when they'd first met. Lemuel sat up taller and looked everyone in the eye. There was a comforting peace about him that hadn't been there before.

He would miss the Beacheys. But Betsy would do as her father wanted, and so would Micah. He would not be the reason the Beacheys were financially crippled, and if he had to sacrifice for Candace, he would. Micah held in a sigh and concentrated on singing to Gött and devoting himself to prayer for the next several hours.

Bishop Mark related his words of faith, and while Micah's soul was at peace, his heart was in pieces. When church concluded and everyone was stirring to leave their seats and go for refreshments, the bishop stopped them with an upturned hand.

"If I could have your attention for one more moment. We have an unorthodox announcement, but when we tell you the details you'll understand." Betsy's father looked over at him.

Micah guessed it was time. He took a deep breath and was about to stand up when Amos beat him to it.

"I would like to say a few words."

There was a shocked murmur through the crowd. It was hard to keep a secret in this small town. Micah was pretty sure everyone knew he had been about to announce his engagement to Betsy. He couldn't help the flash of anger that coursed through him. He didn't want to see Amos announce his engagement to Candace. Although, he supposed fair was fair. After all, Amos would have to watch Micah announce his engagement to the girl Amos wanted to marry. But Micah did feel a little betrayed that Amos hadn't mentioned anything to him.

Micah risked a glance at Candace. She looked horrified. What if she said no? He looked down at Lemuel and Simon. Simon looked uneasy, but Lemuel regarded Amos thoughtfully.

"Oh, of course," the bishop said, clearly as befuddled as everyone else. "Go ahead, Amos."

"A-as you said, this is rather unorthodox. Usually this is done in October and the deacons would announce the names of the brides-to-be.

But in this case," Amos continued with a gesture at Micah, "my cousin Micah needs to get married right away because he is being considered for a deaconship back in Autumnfield."

There was a happy murmur throughout the crowd. Micah smiled in acknowledgement, even though he had no idea where Amos was going with this. It occurred to him that this was the most he'd ever heard Amos speak in one sitting.

"And you may have noticed that the Millers have made a special feast for us after church today. That is to celebrate their daughter, Betsy's, engagement. But there will be two engagements announced today."

Here it comes, Micah thought. He didn't know what to hope for. He didn't want his cousin to be hurt by Candace's refusal. But he also didn't want her to say yes. She was biting her lip nervously. What would she say? It was selfish to want her to refuse, but he didn't think he could handle any other answer.

Amos took a deep breath. "I don't mean to steal his thunder, but I wanted to announce our engagement first and the reason why will be apparent in a few moments." He cleared his throat. "I, Amos Eicher, have proposed to Betsy Miller, and she has accepted me."

Among a collective gasp, Betsy rose from her seat on the other side of the church and nodded. "Ja, I have. I am happy to marry Amos Eicher and live the rest of my life with him by my side." She sat down again.

Micah whipped his head from one to the other. The bishop's face turned an angry shade of red.

"Your turn," Amos said, clapping him on the shoulder, as if he hadn't just thrown the entire congregation into chaos.

Amos meant well, but he didn't know that if Micah didn't marry Betsy, Candace's family wouldn't be able to pay their medical bills. He couldn't even look at Candace right now. His father was also turning an unhealthy shade of purple.

But before Micah could stand up, Lemuel rose to his feet. "Since we're doing this, I might as well throw my hat in the ring as well."

Wait. What?

"As you all know, I've had a hard time since my wife, Sarah, died. It's been a rough road where I almost lost my faith, my family, and my community. It took almost losing another Sarah, my beautiful granddaughter, for me to realize that my wife wouldn't have wanted me to become a bitter old man, disengaged from this life. I don't want to be alone and without companionship. I don't claim to be full of the passion of youth. I'm far too old for that. What I want is kindness, friendship, and a good woman, and to live within the community that has always supported us." He shot a glare at Bishop Mark.

There were a few murmurs throughout the church.

"So, if Judy Eicher will have me as her husband, I would be honored to spend the rest of my life with her."

Judy stood up, fists on her hips. "You're supposed to ask me *alone*. Not in front of the whole congregation."

Lemuel shrugged. "Then say nee."

"Oh no, you don't. I'm also tired of being alone. You're not getting out of this that easily. Ja, we're getting married too."

Micah glanced at Simon, who looked as shocked and dazed as he felt.

"It's your turn," Amos said, elbowing him.

Micah didn't dare turn to look at his father. He got to his feet on wobbly knees. He was supposed to become a deacon and have inspiring words and insights. His head was still reeling because he knew why Lemuel had asked Judy to marry him. Lemuel must have known that Candace didn't want to leave him alone. Now she wouldn't have to.

If Candace agreed to marry him, she could go with him right away to Autumnfield without having to worry if anyone was looking after her father. And if he was chosen as deacon, he would need land and a farm. His father wouldn't want to lose regard in their community by not helping his deacon son.

But he could still demand that Micah become a farmer instead of a woodworker to get the land. Otherwise, they would be stuck living with his parents or one of his brothers. If he had Candace, he could become a farmer. He'd do whatever it took to provide for her.

It still didn't change the fact that the outstanding hospital bills would need to be addressed at some point. But they would figure it out. Maybe since Betsy had agreed to marry Amos, Micah was off the hook. He slid a look at Bishop Mark and was almost blistered by his glare. Or maybe not.

He opened his mouth and Candace stood up, nodding her head. She beamed at him, and suddenly he wasn't nervous anymore. It was as if the entire congregation had faded into the background. It was just the two of them. Micah wasn't exactly sure how all of this would work out, but it would.

"I, Micah Zehr, would like to announce my engagement to Candace Beachey. We plan to be married as soon as possible so we can go back to Autumnfield as husband and wife. If that's all right with you?" he asked her.

Her eyes filled with tears. "Ja, of course."

"Congratulations to the three brides-to-be," Ezekiel said, finally finding his voice. "Now, let's celebrate with the wonderful food and drink the Millers have provided for us."

That broke the spell, and the congregation stood up and began moving. The bishop and his wife stormed out of the room, but only Micah seemed to notice.

Micah barely felt the handshakes and claps on the back as he made his way across the room to Candace, who was hugging Betsy and crying with great, gulping sobs.

Micah faltered, not understanding why she was so upset. But then he got closer and her face cleared. She halted just shy of throwing herself into his arms, but she swayed, and he had to catch her so she didn't fall. *Just like when we met.*

He looked again at his father, who was staring at him, stone-faced. Suddenly, he knew the answer. Perhaps he'd known it all along. He didn't have to be a deacon. He didn't have to have land or money his rich father provided to him. He needed to be his own man.

And he needed Candace.

"We will find a way," Candace said, breathlessly.

"I'm still not on board with the goat yoga," he admitted. "But I know our place is here in Randolph, not in Autumnfield."

"I'll marry you anywhere," Candace said, with a wide smile.

Epilogue

One year later.

Candace looked up into the sky from the porch of her studio next to the home where she'd grown up. She wondered if her mother was looking down from heaven and shaking her head. In her studio, which was right next to the workshop her father and husband shared, fifteen Englischers were doing stretches with seven young goats in pajamas dancing around them.

"I still can't believe people pay money for that." Micah kissed her on the cheek and went out to the larger workshop he and her father had expanded out of necessity.

Esther's medical bills had been completely paid. Once the deacons realized the bishop had been withholding the funds to try to bend others to his will, there had been a series of meetings among the church leadership, with the result that a check had been swiftly written. Mark was still the bishop, but he was being kept in line by the deacons. He had even issued an apology and asked for forgiveness at the next church service.

The Mennonite company that Simon, Micah, and Lemuel had worked for was now using them exclusively for all their cabinetwork. That contract and the additional projects they'd worked on had allowed them to build their savings up once more, beyond what they ever could have hoped for.

And every day Lemuel was a little better. Having a purpose was hastening his recovery. More and more often, he was the Daed Candace had grown up with.

As Candace arranged her soaps and lotions on beautiful wooden shelves Micah had built, Krystal was leading the yoga class with some music that had the sounds of waterfalls and rainstorms interspersed throughout. Krystal's daughter, Kelly, was taking pictures. Kelly would sell them as electronic photographs and email them to the exercising women if they purchased the photo package. That was all beyond Candace. She just rented out the space and they conducted their business there as they saw fit.

Afterward, everyone would get a complimentary bar of honey-almond goat-milk soap and have the opportunity to buy gift baskets and other products. And since they'd gotten their morning workout in, if they wanted to indulge in one of Esther's blueberry muffins or cinnamon rolls, who was she to argue?

Candace's studio was booked every Friday and Saturday morning, as well as Wednesday and Thursday evenings for Krystal's baby goat exercise classes. Once summer hit, they planned to do one morning and one evening class every day except Sundays, and then there was time to pet the goats for any Kinner who came with their parents. Secretly, she hoped they could do more petting-zoo activities. She had her eye on a pair of alpacas and some sheep.

Micah and her father had to finish some custom orders, including one for dining room chairs that one of the women from Krystal's exercise class had ordered a month ago. When they weren't filling orders, they were building up stock for their summer project. Her Daed had the idea to display Adirondack chairs for sale on their front lawn so the Englischers could see them as they drove by and maybe stop to purchase one. And, of course, while they were there, they might as well come and take a look at the goats and the shop Candace had set up in the studio.

Betsy and Amos had stopped by last night with fresh maple syrup to replace what had been sold. Their three-month-old Boppli, named Mark after her father, was colicky, so they couldn't stay long.

Betsy and Amos had gotten married the same day as Candace and Micah. It was a blissful day, and she had been happy to share it with her best friend. Candace often thought Betsy hadn't wanted to wait because she was afraid her father would find a way to marry her off to another suitor.

Amos was doing well for himself as a carpenter. He and his brothers helped out in the workshop when their own shop wasn't packed, creating pieces to sell to the tourists during the warmer months. Betsy had also dropped off some of her coconut cream fry pies. They were so good they'd made the Englisch papers, and now Candace's studio was on "must visit" lists on some New York tourism booklets and websites.

As Candace made her way back toward the house, a horse-drawn wagon bounced up the driveway carrying a load of pine boards and blocks of walnut. It was driven by Ezekiel, who waved to her as he passed by on the way to the workshop. He and his wife, Jerusha, were visiting from Autumnfield, but they were staying at Bishop Mark's house because there was more room and the two men were good friends.

It hadn't been easy, but Ezekiel had come around. Especially when Micah's mother fell in love with Candace's little goats. It had been a rough few months while Ezekiel managed his disappointment, but in the end, he was content that she and Micah were happy. And he had taken her under his wing to help her expand her garden. Their place would never be a big tobacco field or alfalfa farm, but she would be busy canning the garden's bounty this harvest due to his suggestions.

Going inside to check on her rolls, she wondered if she had made enough. She was gathering the materials to make another batch when she heard Gabriel and Abraham come into the kitchen.

"Mamm said to check in with you before going to the workshop," Gabriel said.

"Denki. Can you gather some eggs for me?"

"Ja, and then we can help Grossdaedi and Micah?"

She laughed. "As long as you don't break any eggs."

They ran outside, almost knocking their mother down.

"Walk, boys," Esther called, then set Sarah in the high chair and handed her a toy to play with.

Esther helped Candace in the kitchen while they prepared a big afternoon meal. Judy came by with her boys and brought some casseroles that just needed to be heated up. Judy and her Daed hadn't set a date for their wedding yet. Judy had confided in Candace that the reason her father had stood up that day in church was because he didn't want Candace to turn down Micah because she was afraid to leave him alone. He must have been listening by the kitchen the night Micah and she were talking about it. "We will get married," Judy had assured her. "We're just not in a hurry about it, especially since neither of us can decide where to build the Dawdy Haus—here or on my land."

"Is there a reason for this big get-together?" Judy asked Candace shrewdly when they all stepped outside for a walk around the garden as lunch cooked. Baby Sarah toddled along with them holding her Mamm's hand until she begged Esther to pick her up again.

"I just want to enjoy my family and friends," Candace said innocently. "But I do have something to show you two. Come with me to the studio."

"I still can't believe people pay you to let goats run all over them while they exercise," Judy said, shaking her head.

Candace laughed. "Micah said the same thing, but he doesn't complain about the income." She held the door for the others, and they went into the studio.

The class had just ended, and Krystal and Kelly were finishing the final transactions.

"We're going to need more lavender soap," Krystal called to her.

"I'll have more for you tomorrow," Candace promised.

But she really wanted to show them what was on the magazine rack. Candace handed them each a copy of *Sarah's Best Recipes, A Month of Amish Meals.* "All proceeds will be going to the community medical fund."

"Your Mamm would be very proud of you," Esther said.

"She would be proud of all of us," Judy added, flipping through the book. "Oh, look, her cinnamon rolls are in here. I always wondered what her secret ingredient was." Judy cackled. "Now I know."

"You could have just asked Gabriel," Esther said. "He tells everyone, especially if the word 'secret' is involved."

When they went back outside, each leading a couple of goats on leashes back to the pen, they saw Micah and Simon come out of the workshop carrying a few chairs.

"What are you up to?" Judy asked.

"Well, we just finished Betsy and Amos's kitchen set. Next we're working on nursery furniture," Micah said.

"Micah!" she scolded. That wasn't how she'd wanted to announce that they were expecting a baby.

Esther squealed almost as loud as her daughter. "Congratulations!"

"I was going to tell them after lunch," Candace said, exasperated.

"I already told the other men."

Candace sighed. That wasn't exactly proper. But she loved him for being so proud and excited about the Boppli.

One of the baby goats slipped its leash before Candace could secure it inside the pen. It ran around to Micah, who caught it up and carried it over to Sarah to pet.

"He's going to be a *gut* dad," Esther said.

Candace watched her husband with a full heart. "I know."

"We're working on the crib today," Simon said, kissing his wife on the cheek. "You'll be all right with the kids? Both the two-legged and the four-legged kinds?"

"I'll manage," Esther said, her eyes sparkling.

"Why are the goats wearing pajamas?" Judy asked, cocking her head.

"They're cold. At least that's what Krystal says. I think it's just because the Englischers think they look cuter with them."

Judy nodded. "I could knit a few sweaters for them."

"You and my mother-in-law will get along just fine," Candace said. "She's absolutely enchanted by them. She made all the pajamas they have now."

"I'll be right there," Micah called to Simon. He gently placed the baby goat back into the pen. "When's lunch?" he asked Candace.

Shaking her head, Esther said, "After a year, all the romance is gone."

"You're right. Forgive me." Micah dropped to one knee in front of his wife. "Oh, my light and my treasure! Apple of my eye and song of my heart!" He grinned. "When's lunch?"

"In another two hours, why?" Candace said with a smile.

"I was wondering if we would have time to finish up a bench we've started. It's another one to honor your Mamm and to put in our flower garden."

Candace beamed. He was so thoughtful. "I think lunch can wait until it's done. Or you can take a break to eat and then go back to it. Denki. It's a lovely idea."

"I take it back, there *is* still some romance," Esther said, sniffling.

"I love you, Micah Zehr," Candace said, not caring who heard.

He stood and kissed her. "I love you too, Candace Zehr."

Up to this point, we've been doing all the writing. Now it's *your* turn!

Tell us what you think about this book, the characters, the plot, or anything else you'd like to share with us about this series. We can't wait to hear from *you*!

Log on to give us your feedback at:
https://www.surveymonkey.com/r/HeartsOfAmish

Annie's FICTION